Thomas Gray, Philosopher Cat

Thomas Gray, Philosopher Cat

Philip J. Davis

Illustrated by

Marguerite Dorian

HARCOURT BRACE JOVANOVICH, PUBLISHERS

Boston   San Diego   New York

Library of Congress Cataloging-in-Publication Data
Davis, Philip J., 1923–
Thomas Gray, philosopher cat.
Bibliography: p.
I. Title.
PN6162.D375   1988   813'.54   88-7216
ISBN 0-15-188100-6
Designed by Joy Chu

Printed in the United States of America
First edition   A B C D E

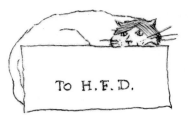

To H.F.D.

Lumen semitis meis

Ps. CXIX.105.

As Coelius was wont to say, that being free from his Studies and more urgent waighty affaires, he was not ashamed to play and sport himselfe with his Cat, and verily it may be called an idle mans pastime.

—EDWARD TOPSELL,
*Historie of Foure-Footed
Beastes,* 1607.

Contents

Arrival

Discovery

Triumph

Angst

Resolution

*I*ntroducing *Thomas Gray*, a cat, and *Lucas Fysst*, a slightly eccentric Fellow of Pembroke College. Their collaboration leads them both to high honours in the intellectual world, and, as an aftermath, raises a number of metaphysial questions.

---

*P*laced in Cambridge, England, this fantasy contains an introduction to the English University scene, an old Irish poem, a still older problem in mathematics, and six meals, together with some speculations on the human condition.

Arrival

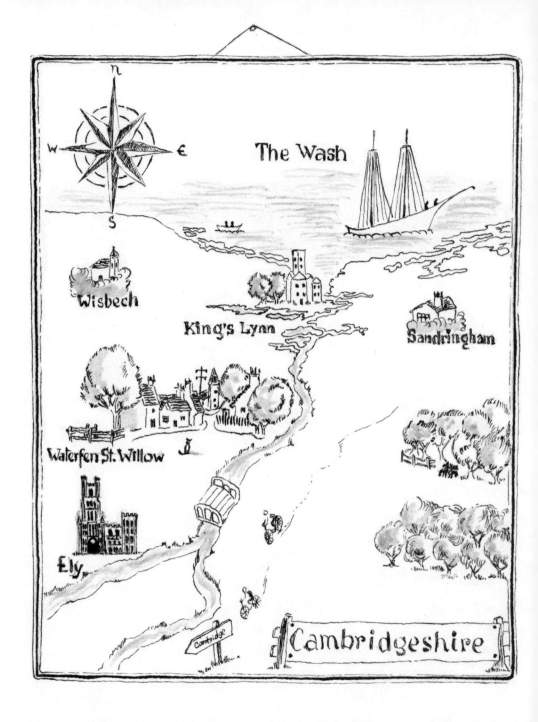

The Wash

Wisbech

King's Lynn

Sandringham

Waterfen St. Willow

Ely

Cambridge

Cambridgeshire

I

How Thomas Gray Came to Cambridge

Thomas Gray, the Pembroke College Cat, was not descended from a long line of Cambridge cats as was the Huxleys' cat or the Thomsons' cat. She was born (yes, *she*; and that's a part of the story) in a litter of five in the small East Anglian village of Waterfen St. Willow in the fenland of England. The English fens are a low, swampy, peaty land, crisscrossed by many small rivers and canals, sparsely populated by people, and not entirely ideal for cats whose negative attitude toward water is well known.

After Thomas Gray was weaned and had a-chieved a certain measure of independence, she went for an interview with the local jobs counsellor, a fat but somewhat Machiavellian grimalkin by the name of Mevrouw. Mevrouw was called Mevrouw not because that was the sound she characteristically

made (which it was), but because she was descended from a Dutch
cat who had come to the area in the Seventeenth Century when
her owners were hired to drain the fens and construct canals and
sluices. Gastarbeiter, in today's parlance.

Mevrouw roused herself from her goosefeather bed and ad-
ministered a battery of tests designed to discover vocational
strengths and weaknesses.

"What is the largest number you know?" she asked Thomas
Gray. At the time, Thomas Gray was not called by that name,
but for the sake of simplicity, let it go at that. (The name was
acquired later in a manner that will be explained.)

Now Thomas Gray knew the number four, and she knew
that she knew the number four. After all, four was the number
of souls she observed in her litter. The word 'souls' is used met-
aphorically, of course. (Do cats have souls? This was a deep question of Mediaeval Theology, and still comes up from time to
time.) She knew that two plus two made four and knew it in a
deep way. She also knew that this knowledge was commonplace
among her contemporaries and that she had better come up with
something with more snap. So she answered Mevrouw, "The largest
number I know is one more than the largest number you know."

"An excellent answer, if a bit paradoxical," Mevrouw replied. But in her heart she said something rather different: This
kid is a wise guy. I'd better get rid of her. For peace and quiet
in the community, naturally.

Mevrouw also realized, not logically, but intuitively, that
this brat from the fens had put her paws on the notion of mathematical variables and had stuck her claws into the tension that
exists between mathematical definition and mathematical existence.

"That completes the intelligence test," Mevrouw said. "Let
us now proceed to the personal interview. What are your life-

aspirations?" she asked, making sure that she got the hyphenation across by an appropriate voice stress.

Thomas Gray answered:

"I do not mean to belittle the Village of Waterfen St. Willow, nor the population thereof. They are the salt of the earth and all that, but I perceive that if I remain here, my life will be one of rats, eels, ducks, and the occasional gull; marriage, of course, a litter or two or three or four.

"For excitement, there would always be the possibility of hiring out as a familiar to one of the queer fen humans or as an acolyte in one of their strange rituals. In the real old days and in remote lands, say in the land of the Sabaeans, when a spirit entered a cat's body, the body would go rigid as an indication. Its head would be chopped off and then it would speak and prophesy. But these days, of course, heads are no longer severed and prophecy is respectable only when it is clad in mathematical rhetoric.

"I don't mind the odd mousing job. As they say, if you have a skill, you must use it or lose it. But as far as the traditional feline professions are concerned, I think 'Ich bin für etwas bessers geboren'. Which I gather is Dutch for 'Smart cats deserve high paying jobs'."

"You've been misinformed as to the language," said Mevrouw, "but no matter. I think you've got a fair grip on the possibilities of feline life in Waterfen St. Willow.

"On the basis of your intelligence test and your interview, I should like to suggest that you hightail it immediately out of this community and go to Cambridge. Your test shows great aptitude for mathematics and in Cambridge you will find mathematicians of superb skill.

"You will find that in Cambridge some believe the mathematical Key to the Universe has just been or is about to be found.

You will also find that in Cambridge the spirit of Wittgenstein hovers over Almost Everything. And if, by luck, his Spirit should possess you, you should then be able to take hold of any number of metaphysical issues that are quite clear and make them rather complicated."

So Mevrouw put Thomas Gray on the next barge going up the Cam, and after several transfers, easily executed, Thomas found her way into Cambridge, entering regally in a punt, like Cleopatra. She leaped out on Silver Street and walked down Trumpington Street and into the great quadrangle of Pembroke College.

2

How Thomas Gray
Got Her Name

*T*he University of Cambridge is one of the oldest and most distinguished in the world. Pembroke College, which is part of it, one college among many, was established in 1347. Within the precincts of Pembroke are to be found undergraduates, Fellows, porters, cooks, waiters, secretaries, bedmakers, handymen, ducks, gardeners, an extraordinary library of ancient books now read by no one, and a wine cellar containing, at the very least, forty thousand bottles of wine and twenty thousand bottles of port. There is also a chapel by Christopher Wren, the first of his designs to be executed, and a Victorian clock tower, quite handsome and reminiscent of Big Ben, but unfortunately neglected on picture post cards in favor (sorry, favour) of bemossed bricks with archaeological aspirations.

At the time of our story, this small kingdom was ruled firmly and wisely by the Master of Pembroke College, Lord Eftsoons

(Ian Dunbar, actually). Lord Eftsoons was also, quite coincidentally, the Vice-Chancellor of the entire University, a post that he was glad to have and that he claimed he would also be glad to relinquish. When asked how he managed to keep so many balls in the air simultaneously, he was inclined to answer, "Magnificently".

The Bursar of Pembroke was one Roderick Haselmere, M.A., who with thrift and devotion watched over its pounds and pence. The Head Porter of Pembroke and Keeper of the Gate was H. J. Stevens, an accommodating man who kept his radio tuned to the racing results. Now, therefore, there abide these three: the Master, the Bursar, and the Porter. And of these, the greatest (in the pragmatic sense) was the Porter.

One bright morning, a meteorological event of considerable rarity in Cambridge, Roderick Haselmere made his way through the outer arch of Pembroke, through the inner arch past the dining hall, and up to his office on the first floor (second floor for American readers). There, waiting for him as though by appointment, was a young cat.

Thomas Gray was suffering a bit from barge lag. She was hungry, but was by no means down at the heels; in other words, to the critical eye of Roderick Haselmere, she appeared to be a perfectly respectable cat. The Bursar was a kindly man and sent down to the kitchens for a dish of milk; he thought that perhaps with this bribe, the cat would go away. The cat did not go away. The cat seemed perfectly at ease in the hallway; she snuggled down in a corner and went to sleep. In the early afternoon, the cat awoke and gave the secretaries on the ground floor to understand that she was hungry and would appreciate a bit of something to keep body and soul together.

"Take her over to Peterhouse," suggested one of the secretaries, alluding to the oldest College at Cambridge, just across the street, "I've heard that they could use a few cats over there."

H. J. Stevens, the Head Porter, was contacted, and the deed was done, surreptitiously. But within a half hour the cat was back at the Bursar's staircase and rather more hungry than before. The Bursar rang up the Head Cook, who sent over a dish of Ragout Montmorency which was then simmering on a low flame. This dish did not please the cat, and there was a feeling of consternation. Recalling the incident many months later, the Head Cook asserted authoritatively that a cat could not be allowed to set standards for High Table. The Bursar remained cool and personally walked up Trumpington Street to Smiley's High Class Provisions and bought the cat a box of Kittikid, which is the feline version of steak and kidney. This pleased her, thank you very much indeed.

The long and the short of the matter was this: the cat moved into the Bursar's staircase on a permanent basis and was fed by the Bursar's Staff. A line item for her maintenance was placed under "Miscellaneous", and was approved by the College Financial Subcommittee at their very next meeting.

The cat exhibited enormous zest for university life and explored the environs of Pembroke College quite thoroughly. She was given to walking up Trumpington Street and Kings Parade, past Fitzbillies' Pastry Shop, past the Copper Kettle cafeteria, all the way to Market Hill, where she was occasionally observed queueing up at the fish stall. She found her way through the great gate at Trinity and into its noble library. Always, by two in the afternoon, she was back at the Bursar's staircase, fast asleep in her corner.

She was a favourite with the undergraduates, but more than that, she was soon noticed by the constant stream of tourists who poked their heads into the ancient archway to gaze politely at the ancient structures that surrounded the quadrangle. Of course, the tourists would ask H. J. Stevens, the Porter, what her name was. The Porter could only admit that the cat bore no name, and this chagrined him greatly. Perhaps he was operating within the racing context where the thought of an unnamed animal would be unsettling. Realizing that the Naming of Cats is a difficult matter—it isn't just one of your holiday games—he suggested to a group of undergraduates that they come up with something appropriate.

The students, who were well versed in Pembroke history, thought of Edmund Spenser, the author of the *Faerie Queene*, who had been at the College. They considered William Pitt the younger, Prime Minister at the age of twenty-five, another Pembroke man. One student suggested that in Elizabethan England, cats were traditionally given food-related names such as "Greedy-guts" or "Jollypudding", but this possibility was voted down on the grounds that the animal had not yet established its reputation as a Renaissance cat.

The name of Roger Williams, the Pembroke matriculant who sailed West and founded Providence Plantations in New

England, came up. But this suggestion was blackballed because of a number of heterodox overtones.

The students finally settled on the name of Thomas Gray, yet another Pembroke man, though a refugee from Peterhouse. He was the author of the much beloved "Elegy Written in a Country Churchyard". What clinched the matter was that he also wrote an "Ode on a Favourite Cat, Drowned in a Tub of Gold Fish" and that in his interlineations in his copy of Linnaeus, he gave the word for cat in ten languages and provided a succinct description of its personality in Latin.

An objection was raised (it was inevitable) that the cat was gray and white, and mostly white. However, this objection was countervailed by the observation that gray and white is, on average, light gray, just as the weather in Cambridge is, on average, a light drizzle. It was further pointed out that Thomas was a far better name for a cat than either Edmund or Roger or William.

Within four months of this discussion, Thomas Gray, the Pembroke Cat, gave birth to five kittens in the privacy of a bush just outside the Bursar's staircase.

3

At High Table

Word came down to the kitchen that Lord Eftsoons, Master of Pembroke, would like a particularly nice dinner for the following Tuesday Evening. The Head Cook responded appropriately, and the following suggestion was sent up and approved.

PEMBROKE COLLEGE

Dinner   Tuesday Evening

Bouillon Écossaise

Entrecôtes d'Agneau

Courgettes à la Sauce d'Oignons

Betterave au naturel

Pommes de terre, fermière

Chateau Beauséjour-Duffau-Lagarrosse '56

Chateau Lafite Rothschild '73

Crêpes à la Reine Elizabeth II

Word got around that something was up. Lord Eftsoons rarely came to High Table, especially now that he had additional social obligations as Vice-Chancellor. Fellows who had not been seen in the evening since the prime ministry of Edward Heath got their academic robes out of moth balls and booked in for the occasion. Twenty-five diners sat at the long oaken table, set with the College silver, stemware, and napery. The undergraduates at their tables below ate quietly for a change, and the portraits of Pembroke Notables, whose lifetimes together spanned centuries, surveyed the scene from within their frames.

Lord Eftsoons sat as Head of Table, and looked around gravely at his Fellows placed along the table as follows:

Lord Eftsoons
O.M., K.B.E., etc.

Prof. Sir George Martin	Prof. Adrian Longwood-Beach
F.R.A.S., O.B.E.	F.R.S.
Dean Knowlton Wesley	Dr. J. M. D. Redding
M.A., D.D., B.A.C.	
	Roderick Haselmere
	M.A.
. The Salt	
.	.
. Well below The Salt	.
Dr. George Apodictou	Dr. Lucas Fysst
.	.
.	.
.	.

One really need not explain to a sophisticated readership accustomed to dealing with Ideas just who these men were. But it will flesh out matters a bit to note that Longwood-Beach was the then Trumpingtonian Professor of Quadrivial Inquiry and that Dr. Redding had only two weeks prior to the dinner been internationally recognized for his work on quasi-fragments, a theory that is noted for its exquisitely honed logic.

The Master rose and said "Benedictus benedicat" (May the Blessed One bless us), to which the assemblage mumbled "Amen". The servants, in formal attire, then served the soup course.

The diners were well into their lamb when the Master raised his voice.

"Fellows of Pembroke. . .er arghh. As Master and as an anatomist with a not in. . .considerable er. . .reputation, I find it most embarrassing, yes, er er most, that our residentiary fauna

should it be faunum er ah, feline, well, you all know him, err, her, Thomas Gray, has this past week, by an act of. . .parturition, shameless, really, though I've heard it said that in today's world creativity must be accompanied by moral turpitude, played havoc with our ana. . .lytic skills, so to speak.

"What I mean is, I believe the continuing presence of such a large brood acts. . .as. . .how shall I put it. . .an irritating reminder of our diagnostic. . . fallibility and holds us up to some measure of ridicule in the eyes. . .at the mouths of certain not to be mentio. . .one anticipates, of course, in certain quarters a certain. . .Yes."

"Hear, hear."

"I should like, therefore, to suggest, er er, to suggest, not to compel, you understand, no in. . .deed, not to compel, we are after all quite adult. Men of the world and all that. . .arrangements be made, yes certain arrangements . . .here at table to effectuate. . .the immediate removal, well, I'm not suggesting immediate, not immediately, of course, Nature must run Her Course, of course, of the. . .how shall I call them. . .er er kittens."

"Hear, hear."

"Yes. Bite the bullet. Here and now. Easier that way. I should like to suggest, perhaps strongly suggest, that each of us here tonight look deep into our hearts and decide, well at least consider the matter, whether er er. . .each of us, as individuals, you understand, might not volunteer to take home. . .er. . .a . . .kitten?"

"Excellent suggestion. Excellent. Splendid."

"Start close to home, as it were. No discrimination at table. Sir George, what d'ya say?"

"Excellent idea. Master. But my wife ails, you know. Ails. Frightfully. Allergic to most living things. Ha. Present company excepted, naturally."

"Yes, of course. Frightful. Hmmm. Longwood-Beach, what d'ya say?"

"Excellent idea, Ian, but you know the conditions of the Trumpingtonian Chair. *Tempore Edwardus VI.* Totally unencumbered. *Nec sano nec bistro*, if I remember the phraseology. *Nec sano nec bistro*, Ian. Bad precedent for the Chair. Very."

"Null for two", as they say in the world of sports. The questioning continued and the score dropped to null for six, null for seven, and the Master's jaw dropped commensurately.

At that point, an obscure voice was heard to speak up from. . .well, from well below the salt.

"Let the matter not trouble you, Master, I shall consult with Bursar in the morning and shall take effective and humane steps."

"Excellent. Splendid. Dr. . .er er arrghh?"

"Fysst. F–Y–S–S–T: rhymes with diced."

"Yes, of course. Fysst. Dogmatic theology, I believe?"

"History of science, actually, Master."

"Yes, of course. Fysst. History of geology. Well, Fysst, we are all grateful. Very grateful, I can assure you."

The matter no longer troubling Lord Eftsoons, he nodded to the servant to bring the silver ewer and the silver laver. He poured a substantial quantity of water on his napkin and cooled his neck and wiped his brow in a gesture of great relief. He then rose, as did the company. He pronounced the words "Benedictus benedicat" as a final grace. "Amen" mumbled, they all retired to the Senior Common Room for port, Madeira, apples, pears, grapes, digestive biscuits, and conversaziones in small groups.

In due course, Dr. Fysst dealt with the matter. He placed a small ad in the *Cambridge Evening News* offering, gratis, five very attractive kittens to select applicants. He chose Latin as his medium of communication, for, as he told his colleague Dr. J. M. D. Redding somewhat later, he wanted to assure Thomas

Gray that the right sort of environment would be secured for her offspring.

The kittens were snapped up within twenty-four hours. With all ambiguities plastered over, peace reigned again in Pembroke. Thomas Gray occupied her corner of the Bursar's staircase in supreme solitude and recalled the words of Mehitabel the cat to her friend Archy the cockroach, upon the occasion of Mehitabel's delivery of a litter of three:

> these terrible
> conflicts are always
> presenting themselves
> to the artist
> the eternal struggle
> between art and life archy
> is something fierce
> yes something fierce.

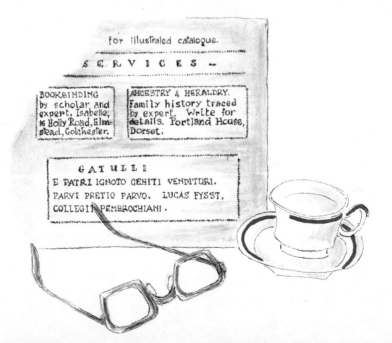

Discovery

4

The Gedankenzoo

Now that her familial duties were discharged, Thomas Gray took to lounging in the common room after lunch and raising her horizons by eavesdropping on the Fellows' conversations. Her presence did not inhibit the Fellows, and they spoke quite candidly.

She overheard much about day-to-day academic concerns, much about personalities, much that had to do with university politics and national politics. She heard a fair amount about who had received offers from America. Quite naturally, she ignored this kind of chatter. Rather more to her taste was gossip about animals, often cats, whose names came up in theoretical or philosophical contexts.

One day, a propos of nothing at all, a Fellow said, "Did you know, Buridan did not write about his *ass*, he wrote about his *dog*. Buridan asserted that when faced with two dishes of food at equal distances, the dog could not find sufficient reason to go either to the one dish or to the other and so the poor animal starved to death."

"If you don't believe that it was a dog," the speaker continued, "I refer you to Buridan's commentary on Aristotle's *De Caelo.*"

"Hear, hear," said a member of the listening circle. "There seems to be a long tradition of asses transforming themselves into other animals. And if you don't believe me you may check it out in Lucius Apuleius's *Metamorphoses of Damned if I Remember What.*"

"Who is Buridan?" asked a Visitor.

"Professor of Philosophy. University of Paris. An Anti-Occamist."

"I think I'll write him for a reprint."

"Around 1330, actually," Lucas Fysst cautioned him.

Thomas Gray's reaction was rather different. She had recently seen a number of ads on the telly for dog food, and after weeks of Kittikid she was now finding her own diet tedious. She could not see, therefore, what the philosophical argument was all about. Of course Buridan's dog (if it was a dog) starved to death; what self-respecting animal would take one step either to the right or to the left in pursuit of a dish of Doggydip?

Rather more subtle was the case of Schroedinger's cat. This animal was referred to by a group of quantum physicists who were sitting around taking coffee. They began by telling Dirac stories. Thomas Gray had already concluded that Dirac stories existed in unlimited supply around Cambridge.

It seems that Professor Paul Adrien Maurice Dirac, St. John's College and Nobel Prize winner, the creator of quantum electro-dynamics, was lecturing one day on this subject. In the course of the lecture he filled the blackboard full of equations. A bright lad, sitting in the first row raised his hand and said, "Professor Dirac, I don't see how you got to the fourth equation from the third."

Professor Dirac thought for while and then answered, "What you have just said was a statement and not a question." And he proceeded with his lecture.

By an unexplained quantum leap, the conversation of the physicists jumped to Schroedinger's cat and the role of the observer in quantum theory. Schroedinger was a famous Austrian physicist. His cat lived in a black box, sharing it with a lethal apparatus that was triggered on a probabilistic basis by beta rays. If the apparatus fired, the cat would be dead; if not, it would be alive.

Now the question was this: if you are not allowed to open the box, how would you describe what is inside it? The average person would say: well, what's inside is either a dead cat or a live cat. But the quantum physicist of the Copenhagen persuasion would say that what is inside is an ensemble of two probability wave functions, the first for a live cat and the second for a dead cat.

Now if an outside observer opens the box and takes a look, he may very well observe that the cat is dead. In that case, the wave function describing the probabilities has collapsed and has been replaced by a certainty.

"Collapsed, man, just collapsed?" asked the Visitor.

Ignoring that interpolation, we may very well ask: Who killed Schroedinger's cat? The observer? And this leads to the deeper question: Can the world be observed without an observer? Does it exist without an observer?

This story did not appeal to Thomas Gray who loved to get into boxes, but would never allow herself to be boxed. And she thought to herself: why did Schroedinger have to put a cat into the black box? Wouldn't it have made as much sense to have jumped into the box himself after asking his colleague Professor Niels Bohr of Copenhagen to describe what would then be inside?

Thomas Gray learned further that whenever physicists used cats to elucidate theoretical points, they called them *Gedankenkatze*, Konceptual Kats, to give the phrase the Gothic appearance it merits. It turned out that Gedankenkatzen played critical roles as actors in what the physicists called *Gedankenexperimente*, dramas of the theoretical imagination, but the language of the physicists was so vivid and so closely reasoned that Thomas could never tell whether they were talking about real or fictitious animals.

One day, Wittgenstein's lion "walked" into the Common Room. Not a cat, exactly, but certainly a close relation. Wittgenstein's lion spoke, and the problem was would anyone understand him?

"What I mean is," said the speaker, "if the lion spoke and no one understood him, could this properly be described as speaking?"

"It depends upon the intentionality of the lion—in the sense of Husserl," piped Sir George Martin from over by the window.

"The nationality of the lion was British, of course. What else?"

"Har bloody har," Sir George said, in a cutting tmesis.

"Who was Wittgenstein?" asked the Visitor.

"Philosopher. I think Russell brought him over here from the University of Vienna."

"I'll call him up for a reprint. What College?"

"Dead, you know."

"But what did Wittgenstein mean?" asked another auditor.

"We don't know, really. The problem is this. Did Wittgenstein himself ever speak, and if he did speak could anyone understand him?"

"Ha bloody ha," echoed Dr. George Apodictou.

Thomas Gray listened to this cheerful chatter and thought to herself that the cats of Waterfen St. Willow and those native to Cambridge were almost entirely incomprehensible to one another; and if that is the case, how on earth should a cat be expected to understand these Common Room subtleties?

And then Whitehead's turtle arrived.

Brought in by an honest young lad from the country who wanted to take his pet along when he rode the train to visit his Aunt in London.

He asked the man at the ticket window how much a ticket for the turtle would be.

The man looked puzzled. He scratched his head. Then the ticket agent consulted Bradshaw. There he found what he wanted and smiled.

"Well now, it seems that a dog's a dog; a cat's a dog, a parrot's a dog and this turtle's a hinsect and goes free."

After telling this story with sufficient gusto to propel him into a repetition of the punch line, Professor Sir George Martin added, "Of course, Professor Alfred North Whitehead used this story as a prolegomenon to his remarks on the Problem of Universals. It's still useful today. Yes, it's useful. Whitehead must have picked it up from Punch."

But Thomas Gray merely thought: a turtle IS an insect and anyone that calls a cat a dog, whether it's Professor Whitehead or Professor Anyone Else, is also an insect and there's an end to the matter.

The parade of gedanken animals went on and on around the Common Room until they constituted a zoo.

The fish of the Chinese Master Chu Ang Tzu swam in one day, initiating an aquatic section.

It seems that Chu Ang and his Disciple were walking together along a river bank.

"The fish in the river are happy," said the Master.

"How can you tell that, Master, considering that you have never been a fish?"

"How can you tell that I have never been a fish, O Disciple, considering that you have never been the Master?"

Fish stories of whatever sort are always comforting, thought Thomas Gray; but that evening, as she dreamed, these famous animals were joined by the abstract unicorn, the manticore, the phoenix, and the basilisk, who had been referred to after lunch by the College Mediaevalist, and together they danced a dance of such violent metaphysical doubt in Thomas Gray's brain that her whiskers twitched furiously until nine o'clock the following morning and she fasted until noon by way of purgation.

5

Her Conscious Tail

*T*he devoted readers of this memoir will by now have checked out what Thomas Gray, the poet, said of his favourite cat who drowned in a tub of gold fish. In the unlikely event that there are some readers who do not keep an anthology of verse on their night table, let me point out that the phrase "her conscious tail", used as the title of this chapter, is from Gray's own description of a late, beloved animal.

By one of those strange turnabouts in the history of ideas, it is now the case that religious faith and devotion can just as frequently be found in the ranks of scientists as in the ranks of seminarians, who may confuse theology with social anthropology. Such a man was Dr. Lucas Fysst, Fellow of Pembroke College and an ordained Anglican priest. Fysst had for his cure not souls, but the history of ancient mathematics. In this field he was preeminent and his conclusions were cited as authoritative.

Dr. Fysst was, of necessity, a great linguist; he picked up languages as a dog tramping through the October woods picks up thistle burrs. In addition to the principal contemporary European languages, Dr. Fysst could read Latin, Greek, Arabic, Sanskrit, Persian, Ancient Egyptian, and Coptic. His theological training had given him Hebrew and some Aramaic while his purely recreational accomplishments in the language line included Anglo-Saxon, Celtic, Welsh, and Cornish.

Lucas Fysst was a bachelor and lived in College. He was inclined to a rather rigid interpretation of religious belief; that is, he did not espouse the metaphorical or psychoanalytical — these were a dilution of meaning — but asserted that an angel was an angel; and a devil, a devil in the strict and literal sense of the words. He wore variously, according to some inner ecclesiastical calendar of his own devising, tweeds and a collar or Levis and a collar, and he was often seen playing a formidable game of cricket in cassock and cleated cricket shoes, with his skirts flying behind him.

Fysst abhorred the telly, despised the wireless, but had a record player on which he played music no later than that of Pergolesi (1710–1736). He ate frugally, drank the occasional glass of wine, and was inordinately fond of Evensong, a service at which he often officiated. He smoked the occasional pipe, pro forma, but not cigarettes; and he induced no elevated states of mind by means either of cannabis or starvation. His bedtime reading and rereading and rereading was Wilkie Collins laced with the *Acta Concilii Constanciensis, 1414–1418.* The latter document was in four volumes, but since it lay well away from his direct professional interests, he regarded it as light entertainment; the Latin text detailing how the Council of Constance got rid of both John XXIII and John Hus was his equivalent of soap opera.

It might be concluded from this description that Lucas Fysst was of a melancholy, saturnine disposition, but this was not the case. He was generally cheerful; well, let us say, as often as the sun shone in Cambridge, and this cheerfulness he attributed to the fact that he read no newspapers except on December 31st when the summary of the past year was published. *"Gestae Conservatorum,"* he called it, the Deeds of the Conservatives.

Fysst was often heard to remark that nothing elated him so much, nothing sustained him so much in his Emersonian belief in the World as Balanced Tohubohu as the study of the mathematics of the fourth century (A.D.), which was as dismal a period for this science as it was glorious for Christianity.

Into his bachelor quarters one day walked a small gray and white animal of loving disposition and of conscious tail. To put it bluntly, Thomas Gray, in one of her expeditions of exploration and inquiry, invaded Lucas Fysst's rooms and charmed the socks off the solitary scholar with her joyful purring and her unabashed display of affection.

The scholar responded immediately, and in his naiveté, produced several pieces of Weetabix from his cupboard. The cat, quite naturally, spurned these. Proceeding to the other end of the spectrum, Lucas Fysst produced slices of mandarin orange, in a light syrup, and a cube of Turk-ish Delight, items he normally reserved for Seasons of Joy and Thanksgiving. The cat abstained.

It seemed that what she sought was not food, but the exhilaration of pawing through, around, and on top of the mountains of books, journals, and manuscripts that were piled at hazard on his floors, shelves, dressers, sills, washstand, and bed. She was never happier than when she was searching and discovering. He allowed her carte blanche in her research work, though normally he would have screamed had anyone moved the slightest paper from its set position in its chaotic array, and she rewarded him by returning day after day precisely at teatime.

His work went well, and when Thomas Gray was around, he often talked to her and played with her. He loved to sing her a ninth century Irish song about a scholar and his cat:

Messe ocus Pangur Bán
cechtar náthar fria saindán:
bíth a menma-sam fri seilgg,
mu menma céin im saincheirdd.

In English:

Pangur Bán, my cat, and I
Each have private skills we ply;
His is hunting tiny creatures,
Mine relates to ancient teachers.

This rendition is Lucas Fysst's, and, as he himself would allow, the English is only a shadow of the original.

As the weeks went by, the cat became more familiar with Fysst's rooms, and bolder in her relationship with Fysst himself. As he worked away, collating, making lists and glossaries, translating, interpreting, preparing commentary, Thomas Gray would often jump into his lap; or she would proceed from his lap onto his work table and lie down quietly; or even, occasionally, tread on the pages of his precious documents and take a look at the material.

This, then, was the beginning of a friendship, a collaboration, a love affair even, between a scholar and a cat: a collaboration which was to be enormously productive for both and which raised them to undreamed of heights in the small world of classical studies and in the larger realms of intellectual endeavour.

6

The Discovery

The background of their collaboration involved events of the seventeenth century as well as of the twentieth, together with numerous technicalities. Let Lucas Fysst himself describe them:

Where shall I start? Of course, one should always start, *ad majorem Dei gloriam*, with Genesis 1:1, the Creation; but who possesses the wisdom to delineate the strands that will take us back so far? That being the case, I will start with a fairly recent event, *sub specie aeternitatis*. I shall begin in the year 1634, and work both ways: backwards and forwards.

In that year, a cornerstone was being laid for a new wing of the Bodleian Library at Oxford. The event was one of ritual splendour. The Heads of Colleges, the Proctors, the Principals, the Vice-Chancellor of Oxford were all present and garbed in their academic regalia. Flags were flying, flowers were set out, and music was laid on. A scaffolding had been erected for the VIPs to sit on. No doubt there would be subsequent gorging

and quaffing. I recall seeing a copperplate of some Oxford wor-
thies of this period and a fat lot they were.

What occasioned the new wing was that a large and first-
class collection of manuscripts had been donated to the library
and proper housing was wanted for it.

The Vice-Chancellor stepped forward to place a gold coin in
the cornerstone, as tradition required. Just then, the whole scaffolding gave way, and the VIPs were thrown to the ground bruised,
but not seriously hurt. Blame the contractors if you like. Or the
general embonpoint.

The donor of the manuscripts was a well-born, talented young
man of about thirty by the name of Sir Kenelm Digby. In 1628,

Digby had undertaken a trip for business and pleasure as we would now say. The business part was this: he had been advised that if he wanted to advance his status at Court he ought to go out as a privateer and capture a few ships—richly laden ships, naturally.

The pleasure part was this: Since travel is both education and experience, as Francis Bacon observed, he would increase his wisdom by meeting with wise people and by collecting the wisdom embodied in rare books and manuscripts. In those days it was widely held that a special wisdom, largely forgotten, had been vouchsafed to the ancients, but was recoverable if one were lucky enough to find the right books.

Digby outfitted two ships, hired two captains, and had a considerable success in the harbour of Scanderoon, which is what Alexandretta was often called in his day. As far as collecting ancient material was concerned, he also met with success, for somewhere—possibly in Aleppo—he bought or contrived to assemble (one shouldn't ask too many questions) a substantial library of Arabic books and manuscripts having to do with scientific and mathematical topics.

I interrupt my narrative to say that Digby led one of your more interesting lives. He was a philosopher, an author, and a diplomat. He was an amateur scientist and looked into medical, astrological and mathematical questions. He was a writer and a book collector. One moment he might be writing on questions of doctrinal infallibility and the next moment he would be investigating chicken eggs or optical prisms or collecting recipes for metheglin.

He was a philanthropist in an age when the term had hardly any institutionalized meaning. He was an English Catholic in a period when Charles's head fell under the axe. He suffered greatly during the Commonwealth, and it's important for my story that he did. It's a very ill wind, etcetera.

In all these pursuits, with some few exceptions, Kenelm Digby just missed greatness; he was good, but he wasn't good enough. I like to think that the collapse of the scaffolding can be taken as an augury of his life, in which structures and intentions collapsed without grave catastrophe and in which some goals were attained. And what was attained was such that the larger world hardly sat up, took notice and cried "hurrah".

In 1630, Thomas Allen, a mathematician and Digby's mentor, left him a valuable collection of books and manuscripts, mainly the works of mediaeval scribes. Digby combined Allen's collection with his own, and after consultation with Archbishop Laud, donated the enlarged collection to the Bodleian Library at Oxford.

It was Digby's intention (and it was unusual for his day), that the books he donated to the Bodleian be made available to the general public for reading or for copying. This collection still resides in the Bodleian under the name of *The Digby MSS*, and each item is stamped with Digby's coat of arms or with the initials KD or KVD (*V* for Venetia, his wife, She died early. So young, so lovely and so notorious. Alas.)

Digby promised to make a further donation to the Bodleian, but apparently he never did. He gave Laud some of his Arabic manuscripts to send to the University or to the library of St. John's College, but apparently Laud never did. He sent forty books to the newly-established Harvard College in the Cambridge in New England, and these were destroyed in a fire a few years later.

His own personal library was probably confiscated and burned by the parliamentary government of Oliver Cromwell, for such was the practise of the Roundhead government. Digby was banished from England in 1643 and went to France where he accumulated a second library. When he returned to England after the Restoration, he expected to go back and bring it over. He never did.

After his death, his library in France was declared crown property under an old French law that permitted such a confiscation in the case of an unnaturalized resident. Some of those books are now in the Bibliothèque Nationale. It's very strange, but Digbeiana keeps turning up and turning up all over the world.

A good deal of it, I should think, is suspect. The rare book dealers wink their eyes and make a profit when they can. A few years back a man rang me up, said he was a rare book dealer in London, and would I care to advise him on a parchment that was offered to him. I asked him what it was, and he said it was the secret log book that Columbus placed in a cask and flung into the raging sea when his expedition ran into a storm on the trip home. In case he perished, he wanted his discoveries to be secured. Now all this sounded amusing, so I agreed and the dealer came round the next week.

I must say, the simulacrum was very good indeed. Parchment nicely aged. Some signs of water damage. Writing properly aged. Calligraphy would easily pass for that of the Admiral. The contents entreated the finder to announce to the King and Queen of Spain that the islands of the Indies had been discovered and claimed for Their Majesties. This was followed by a long description of the islands and their inhabitants. The religious motif was prominently displayed (for Columbus was a devout man) and stressed that our Holy Saviour now rejoiced on earth as well as on high for the new abundance of souls that would be saved. In short, all was in apple-pie order, except for a minor blunder.

I told the dealer the document was faked, and he thanked me and walked off without asking for an explanation. Two days later I found a cheque in the mail by way of a consultation fee. It's a nice feeling to be believed without the necessity of having to defend one's beliefs, even though in this case my display of intelligence was minimal: the document was in English. Incredible.

Ah well, forged documents have been with us since antiquity. I suppose it's one of the minor sins. These days it's part of a game. Collectors of rare books have it coming to them. To them, books are either icons or investments. Some dealers hardly know how to read. But even experts can be taken in. My learned historical colleague from a neighbouring college was taken in badly a few years back. Such episodes lend spice to a profession that must seem just a trifle *sec*.

I now skip to the year 1870; I have no knowledge of the intervening years. I've pursued the matter somewhat. I've even been down to the Digby House at Gayhurst and poked around but turned up nothing interesting.

In 1870, J. J. Menzies and Sons, booksellers and auctioneers in the Charing Cross Road, were offered for sale by a "private and anonymous party" a parcel of miscellaneous but rare books that included three manuscripts in Arabic each of which bore the Digby coat of arms. This lot was bought for £100 by the Earl of Fennismere, who was a collector of such things but not particularly interested in their contents. The books were placed in storage in his library and were not taken out of the boxes supplied by Menzies.

Sometime in the late 1930s, the then Earl, who had been an undergraduate here at Pembroke College, had the boxes opened up with a view to donating the books to our library. He held consultations with our librarian, and the books were split into two parts, the first of which was sold off, while the second was shipped here in the original boxes of J. J. Menzies and Sons. The original detailed invoice made out in 1870 was even found.

I'm sorry to say that when the books got to our library they were not all removed from their boxes and catalogued — perhaps World War II interfered. Some were left to gather dust and decay in an obscure corner of the library storage room. The librarian and his assistant both died, as did some of the Fellows who took an interest in the Library, and that is where matters stood until several years ago.

At that time, the College decided to transfer most of its rare book holdings to a central university facility that would be able to keep them under better conditions. They would be on permanent loan, but on loan nevertheless, from Pembroke College. I volunteered to help with this work. It was up my alley, really. For the most part I did it in the late afternoon after I had discharged my tutorial duties and other College obligations. It involved examining books, deciding what was rare and what was not; what would be useful to a working undergraduate and what would not. That sort of thing.

One afternoon, Thomas Gray came over to my study a bit early. I had in mind to put in some time in the Library, and when I walked over there she went with me. As I went about my work, taking books off the shelves and examining them, she poked around in the adjacent storage room, in odd corners and in odd boxes, in piles of old trash, in piles of old examination books. There was nothing she liked better.

One large carton was open; that is to say, the four flaps on top were free. Thomas found her way under them and into the carton. It was dark in that corner of the storage room and doubly dark inside the carton. Thomas scratched around in it trying to get out. I heard the noise and went over. And that is how I found the ibn Kurra manuscript. It bore the Digby coat of arms and that is how I was able to reconstruct its provenance, to the extent that I've been able.

I must say, the discovery sent me into a quite high state of elation. What a piece of luck! How I danced with the cat! But then, in my business, there are many stories of many pieces of luck.

7

The Square Root of Seventeen

he Arabic manuscript was one out of three, remember, and what I wouldn't have given to have found the other two in that box, or even to have been able to find out what happened to them. One must be grateful for what one has. What the librarian in 1932 had in mind when he let the other two manuscripts get away is beyond comprehension. What an opportunity lost! Ah, well.

What my Arabic manuscript was—I call it mine (I've pored over it for quite a while now), but it carries the Pembroke coat of arms and is catalogued—my manuscript turned out to be a tenth century copy of a ninth century translation. It was a translation of part of the lost book of Eudemus of Rhodes called the *History of Geometry* and was prepared by the famous mathematician and descendant of Babylonian star worshippers, Thabit ibn Qurra.

A part of the ancient world of ideas, thought to be lost and sought for centuries, had now come to light. In my manuscript, amongst many other things, Eudemus discusses the sequence of square roots presented by Theodorus of Cyrene. This has been a much-discussed and much-argued topic. It was precisely in the middle of Eudemus's discussion of it that I came across a passage of such difficulty that I couldn't make head or tail of it.

Now comes a part of my story, said Lucas Fysst, that is mathematical. If you don't like mathematics, you may stop up your ears. I shall try to make my recitation as short as I can. Fundamentally, the mathematics is simple; it hardly exceeds what is taught in every high school, though I must say that some of its modern ramifications are indeed deep. The ideas lead to an interesting instance of what modern mathematicians call *gleichver-teilte* or "equidistributed" sequences. I do not myself understand such things. I am primarily a classicist and my knowledge of mathematics stops, more or less, with Newton.

If you take a look at Plato's *Theaetetus* (147 C) you will find there a dialogue between Socrates and Theatetus, a sixteen-year-old boy. They are discussing the generation of general ideas out of specific instances. Theaetetus gives an instance from mathematics by referring to the work of an older mathematician, Theodorus. Theaetetus says (I give a rough translation):

"Theodorus was writing out for us something about square roots, such as the square roots of three or of five, showing they are incommensurable with the unit. He selected other examples up to seventeen. There he stopped."

These characters are historical. Theodorus of Cyrene lived from 470 B.C. to 400 B.C. and was Plato's teacher. Theaetetus lived from 417 B.C. to 368 B.C. Both were mathematicians.

I will remind you what incommensurability means. A number such as the square root of two is incommensurable with the unit because it is impossible, demonstrably impossible, to express it as a fraction such as 7/5 or 141/100. Now the square root of two is the length of the diagonal of a square whose side is of length one and hence has palpable existence. But the ancient Greek number system contained only the integers 1,2,3,. . ., and the fractions such as 7/5 or 141/100, created by dividing one integer by another. The Greeks were therefore forced to conclude that the diagonal of the square, which has palpable existence, can have no existence as a measureable quantity. This paradox led to a profound crisis in Greek science and philosophy. Hence anything that relates to the history of incommensurables is of great importance to historians of science.

Historians of ancient mathematics have for many many years asked themselves the question: why did Theodorus stop when he came to seventeen? Beginning in Greek antiquity itself, many words have been written about this question. Now when you first hear the question, you might say to yourself: "What a silly question. Theodorus had to stop somewhere, didn't he; he couldn't go on forever listing the square roots because there are an unlimited number of them."

If you answer the question this way, then you are a companion to many professional mathematicians who feel the same way you do. For example, I've heard that the world famous mathematician Carl Ludwig Siegel dismissed the problem by saying that seventeen was as far as Theodorus had gotten when the lecture hour came to an end. The bell rang on him.

However, there are many other students of the history of mathematics who think otherwise. In the first place, it is known that Theodorus was of the Pythagorean School, and to Pythagoreans, each number had a special, individual, mathematical, but often mystic or religious significance. They conclude, therefore, that there must be a particular significance to the number sev-

enteen that is relevant to the process of constructing incommensurable numbers. What is that significance?

Many answers have been given, based upon inferential evidence and not on direct textual material. The translation of prac-
tically every Greek word of the quotation I just gave you has
been called into question. For example, the phrase "writing out"
might be translated as "indicating by diagrams". The word
"showing" can be interpreted as showing in an intuitive way, or
proving in a rigorous way, or even alluding to such a proof. The
phrase "there he stopped" can also, with some justice, be translated as "there or then he ran into difficulties". Each of these
readings can lead to a different inferential conclusion.

Some years ago, in 1918 to be exact, a German businessman
by the name of J. H. Anderhub, who was an inspired mathematical amateur, suggested very simple, very attractive explanation. Anderhub supposed that Theodorus constructed the lengths
root 2, root 3,. . .by placing right-angled triangles next to each
other, as suggested by the diagram I will now draw.

It is not difficult to deduce, using the famous Theorem of
Pythagoras, that the lengths of the sequence of hypothenuses are
root 2, root 3, root 4, and so on. Now note the way the triangles
form a spiral. Indeed, Prof. Hlawka, in Vienna, refers to this
figure as a "square root snail". You may extend this figure up to
root 17. If you then attempt to extend it beyond, to root 18,
you will find that the new triangle cuts across the first triangle.
After 17 it would get very messy indeed. What Anderhub was
saying, therefore, is that seventeen is the greatest integer to pro-
duce a neat or a non-self-overlapping figure.

Now this conjecture as to why Theodorus stopped at seventeen is, after all, merely a conjecture. And although it is an
attractive solution, it has been called into question. Many scholars have tried to solve the problem by tying in their explanation

to the manner in which Theodorus was supposed to have demonstrated the incommensurability of root 2, root 3, and so on. They have provided answers along these lines, some of them quite convincing, but I shall pass over them.

Some scholars, purists really, insist on direct evidence and deprecate all reconstructions and conjectures. Ancient documents do not shed much direct light on the problem. But now that I have made sense out of the manuscript of Thabit ibn Qurra which is a translation of a lost commentary of Eudemus, I know that Anderhub's solution is very likely the correct one. Well, at least that is the opinion of Eudemus.

Eudemus talks about the square root snail. Of course he doesn't call it that and he doesn't have a diagram. Then comes the passage I struggled with. It consists of three successive lines of Arabic one on top of the other in a narrow column. First line: "sixteen, the quadratic feet of seventeen". Second line: "he explained it this way the quadratic feet of eighteen". Third line: "and so he stopped".

Feet. Yes, *feet*, not root, for feet is the word in the original Greek. There's no difficulty in feet. But the passage as a whole had me stopped cold.

I was working over this passage for perhaps the hundreth time. Thomas Gray was on my worktable, when the following thing happened. She threw her tail over the manuscript, and momentarily, the words "he explained it this way" were deleted. And then I saw vividly that the words for root 17 overlapped the words for root 18. I interpreted this as Eudemus's verbal or orthographical way of indicating a graphical overlap when a figure is drawn.

Words that some scribe had interpolated into Eudemus' text for the purpose of clarification had only served to confuse me terribly, and not until Thomas deleted the interpolation did I see the meaning.

I wrote this up as a short paper, pointing out places in ancient mathematics where this kind of orthographical – graphical substitution occurs, and sent it off to the Archive for Ancient Science for publication. I gave full credit to Thomas Gray for her insight, and trumpeted her brilliance around Pembroke. Her reputation spread to the whole University.

The work I am doing now consists largely of preparing a critical edition of the Thabit ibn Qurra manuscript. The discussion of the problem of Theodorus actually occupies only a few paragraphs. When my work is published, it is my firm intention to include a dedication page, in Arabic, to Thomas Gray.

8

Sonata Appassionata

Lucas Fysst, scholar and scientist that he is, has given us a dry, objective, passionless version of his great discoveries. There is another version, short and warm, that reveals another side of the man.

On that afternoon in late October, Lucas Fysst pushed his chair aside momentarily to get up and prepare himself a cup of tea and a bowl of Weetabix. He was quite happy and as he went out to the refrigerator in the hall, he sang a post-Pergolesi lyric of his own devising to a traditional tune:

Just a bowl at twilight
When the lights are low
And the sliced bananas
Softly come and go. . .

Thomas Gray was lying on the work table and saw this as an opportunity to move to a more central location. In the course of her manoeuvre, she spread her tail over the problematic passage. Lucas returned to his table and resumed work. He looked again at the Arabic text and within a few short seconds he burst out:

"Eureka. Eureka. I've got it. Yes, I've got it. Ich hab's gefunden, verstehst du mich? Oh, thou sweet cat. Thou wise and noble cat. Thou perspicacious cat. Oh Pangur Bán, be exalted above all other cats and thy conscious tail be exalted above all other tails; for it is the sword wherewith I have cut through the darkness. Matzati, matzati! List, oh list, while I make a joyful noise unto the Lord. Bring hither the timbrel, the harp, and the psaltery. Tra tra ta tra."

Lucas Fysst caught Thomas Gray up in his arms, calling her his Pangur Bán and danced around the room with her whilst singing the Gaelic version of

> Pangur sees a mouse's venture,
> Joyful then his pounce to clench her!
> Joyful am I when obsessed
> By classic puzzles readdressed!
>
> Pangur Bán within his space
> Catches mice with feline grace;
> I pursue my studies deep
> And love the quiet hours I keep.

The frightened cat struggled to get loose. She jumped to the floor and from there to the sill of an open window. And from the sill, she jumped out to the quadrangle where she disappeared around a corner.

Triumph

9

Private Languages

ypothecating the Queen," said Dr. J. M. D. Redding to his colleague Dr. Lucas Fysst one afternoon as they were strolling along the Cam in the vicinity of the boat houses, "all else follows."

"Surely, John, you meant to say 'hypothesizing the Queen'. I fail to see how, Old Boy, except in a hostage situation, the Queen could be hypothecated."

"Sorry. Of course. Silly error. Hypothesizing the Queen, all else follows. By that I mean that each of us contains in our individual physical and mental being the whole universe. Given the Queen, the whole universe, its past and its future could theoretically be constructed out of her. The macrocosm resides in the microcosm."

"And if in the Queen, surely in the cat. What could distinguish the two cosmogenically?"

"What, indeed," responded John Redding, "and speaking of cats, I hear you've had a smashing success in your collaboration with Thomas Gray."

"Yes, quite."

"The World Has Sat Up and all that?"

"Well, let us say the world of classical scholarship."

"Would you say he's 'O levels' equivalent?"

"She. Easily. Of course, one must remember that the private ideational space of Thomas is rather different from that of you or me. One cannot translate on the basis of a one-to-one, idea-to-idea correspondence."

"Quite. Would you say he had 'A levels' competence?"

"She. Very likely. She's a cat in a million. She can go all the way."

"The reason I ask, Padre, is that I have a theory of private languages I should like to test out. I should like to use Thomas Gray as a subject. Could you set it up for me?"

"Nothing easier. Come to my room at teatime. She's generally around. Bring some chocolate or something like that. The way to her heart is by offering her something she's sure to turn down. Gives her a chance to feel independent."

So a date was set up and Lucas Fysst found an excuse to absent himself. J. M. D. Redding gave out a preliminary report a few days later.

"I started by reading poetry. Standard, well-known things. Shakespeare's sonnets. The Romantics. Tennyson. Swinburne. Gerard Manley Hopkins. No reaction. None whatsoever."

"You did the Metaphysicals, of course? Surely she would have reacted to Donne."

"No reaction there. And then, strangely, coming closer to our own time, I got to the Imagists, and there, I noticed that a pronounced twitching of the whiskers set in."

"Boredom, possibly. I mean with the test, not with the poems."

"Possibly. I shall repeat the experiment in a few days, changing the order of the various genres."

"Yes. One should randomize."

At their next encounter, Redding reported further "successes."

"Changed the order of the readings completely; again a twitching when we came to the Imagists."

"What do you make of it?"

"Too early to say. I want now to leave poetic expression completely and go over to mathematics. After all, that's where you were operating with her."

Dr. Redding's thinking went along the following lines. The number that mathematicians call pi (usually written as the Greek letter π) inheres in the universe. Pi is the length of the circumference of a circle whose diameter is one unit. But pi has many, many other equivalent interpretations and representations. It is one of the fundamental numbers running through the whole of mathematics.

In the decimal system, the value of pi is 3.14159. . .and this value has been computed out to several hundreds of millions of decimal places. Insofar as pi is a fundamental object of mathematics, and insofar as mathematics is itself totally abstract, with an objective existence claimed to be independent of humans, pi exists equally well in atoms, in galaxies, in Queens and in cats. It is pan-ontologic. It is immanent.

Dr. Redding tested for the Immanence of Pi in a very bright cat.

He converted the first twenty decimals of pi to the binary system, believing that binary would be less prejudicial to Thomas Gray than decimal. This is a trivial matter on today's computers and the computation gave him a certain sequence of zeros and ones to work with. Specifically, pi in binary is 11.0010010000111. . . .

Redding then subjected the cat to this sequence in the following manner. He got two wine glasses from Fysst's cupboard and filled them at different levels; the first with red wine and the second with white. He then struck the glasses with a knife handle, striking the red glass if the bit in the sequence was a one and the white glass if it was a zero. The tones emitted were, of course, different in each case.

"What happened?" asked Lucas Fysst.

"A pronounced twitching of the whiskers between the fourteenth and the twentieth binary bits."

"You repeated the experiment?"

"Several times over. Same result."

"Did you switch colours, striking the red if the bit was zero and the white if it was one?"

"I did. Same result. Incidentally, Padre, you really ought to stock a better white wine. Your selection is far too sweet. It gives a man the pip."

"I've noticed a rather prevalent and, I must say, rather nasty feeling among those who prefer a dry wine that to prefer a sweet wine is an indication of ethical cretinism."

"You suggest that a sweet wine is morally defensible? Well, let's get back to the experiment, shall we?"

"You eliminated the possibility of cueing on your part?"

"I set up a blanket as a screen and tinkled the glasses from behind it. I observed the cat through a moth hole."

"Moth? Good thinking. And what do you make of it?"

"The existence of private languages is confirmed. The existence of public languages is confirmed. The existence of universal languages is confirmed. The relationship between the three is enormously complex and deserves much study. One thing is clear. Thomas Gray is no ordinary cat."

"I always thought so, and I've told her as much," said Lucas Fysst.

10

George Entertains
a Lady

A t 4:41 of a Tuesday afternoon, Daphne Dhu, née Durogi Dorottya, star of Cal-Ouse Productions, a subsidiary of the Alpha-Omega Group, drove up the narrow streets of Cambridge to the Garden House Hotel and allowed the desk clerk to deal somehow with her creamy white Rolls Royce.

The same Tuesday evening, Daphne Dhu swept into the dining room of the Garden House on the arm of Dr. George Apodictou. All eyes in the dining room turned to the couple as Daphne's skirts swished and her very high heels clicked.

One may very well ask how it came about that a Reader in Byzantine History and Literature was acquainted with a young lady—well, perhaps not so young—whose name was synonymous on two continents for effervescent pulchritude. The answer is simple: George was Daphne's first cousin once removed and her favourite such cousin; and she wanted to talk to him about her career.

Dr. George Apodictou was a man of many worlds including the real world. Born on the Island of Corfu of a Greek father and a Hungarian mother, he grew up principally in London. He was sharp as a needle, impatient, and often ecstatic in his enthusiasms. When he wasn't playing bridge—and he was a master player—he was looking into a particular nineteenth century reconstruction of tenth century Ukranian history. His professional interests occasionally overlapped those of Lucas Fysst, and the two had become friendly.

At the time of the Troubles with the Greek Colonels, George was a student at Oxford, and his native patriotism came to the surface. Along with many students, he picketed the Greek embassy and was thrown into jail. He got an early release due to the behind-scenes effort of a brilliant solicitor whose sister he (George) proceeded to marry.

George's speech was erratic. One moment he spoke pure English, in imitation of the speech of his Hungarian semi-countryman George Sanders, whom women of over sixty will recall as a suave Hollywood heartthrob. The next moment, particularly if he was excited, he might lapse into a strange personal tongue that he himself called Anglou-Apodictou.

All of this is interesting and relevant to George's future biographer, but together with Daphne's curriculum vitae, is totally irrelevant to the scene that is about to unfold. What is relevant is that the precise moment when Daphne said to George, "Freddy wants me to do 'Her Loyal Heart'," and George answered, "Go along with Freddy. What's the problem?" was exactly the moment when Thomas Gray walked into the Garden House dining room and sat down near their table.

"This is Thomas Gray, the cat at Pembroke," said George quite coolly, as though he made a regular habit of introducing cats to ladies in the dining room of the Garden House.

"Gyere ide kis cica; gyere gyere," said Daphne. "Hol votál, cica?"

Thomas Gray to whom all human languages were equal, though some, including Hungarian, were more equal, interpreted this noise as meaning: pussy cat, pussy cat where have you been? The question was patronizing and impugned her independence. She ignored it. Actually, she had been exploring the fens behind Peterhouse and found that romping there assuaged somewhat her homesickness for Waterfen St. Willow.

A waiter approached and Daphne ordered the chicken. George, feeling rather British that evening—he had walked to the Garden House carrying his umbrella even though the skies were perfectly clear—ordered the Lamb Broil together with potatoes and sprouts. When Thomas Gray heard George's order, she put out a powerful miaow.

"On second thought," George said to the waiter, "I'll have plaice. And bring me another plate. I shall want to feed cat."

"Feed the cat, sir? Another PLAICE setting, sir?"

"Ha ha. Excellent. Another plaice setting. Did you hear that, Dorottya?" No response from Daphne.

"THANK you, sir."

"Thank YOU."

"Thank you, SIR."

Daphne talked about Freddy. He was making "Her Loyal Heart" on a shoestring, really. He was hardly able to scrape together three and a half million pounds. He had gotten the idea for the script in a paperback left on a seat on the Northern Line. Daphne complained about her contract and her subsidiary rights. She complained about her part.

George listened. The real problem, he sensed, was that the role of Lady Phyllis Stanhope was too insubstantial.

"I think, Dora, you are complain that part is, how you say, of too much triviality."

"No no no no NO, George. Je suis artiste."

"Bien sur. Indubitable."

Then the food came. George ate and fed the cat in alternation. Daphne poked at her chicken.

"George, are you listening?"

"Do what Freddy wants. I told you definitely advice. Now change subject please. Very fast! Allaxe to thema, kae ghrighora," he emphasized, switching into Greek.

"Do you know what, George?"

"No. What?"

"Do you know that today is my Saint's Day?"

"Oh Dora. I should have remembered. Happy returns. You know you have lasted longer than the Peloponnesian War?"

"I know. I know. And in my case, I wonder who the winner is. Do you know what, George?"

"No. What?"

"I had an overseas call from the Parameter Pantheon in Orlando. They want to simulate my bosom in B-splines for the Pantheon. That's computer geometry talk. Think of that, George, little geometrical me, George."

"I think of your geometry. Constantly I am thinking of it. Believe me."

George ate and fed the cat, who was quite pleased with the fish.

"Do you know what they do then?" Daphne toyed with her chicken.

"No. What they do then?"

"They put my parameters in a data bank. For eternity, George. Are you listening, George?"

"Tell Parameter Bank 'yes'. Perpetual Care for parameters. Is a very good thing. Is like deep freeze."

Thomas Gray jumped on George's lap and ate a bit from George's plate. George encouraged her and she found his place setting rather more soignée than the one on the floor.

"George. Oh, George, you're not listening to me at all."

Daphne dashed her napkin down to the floor in a fury and spat out, "Menj a fenébe, cica". She swished out of the dining room. All eyes followed her.

When she returned from the Ladies, her chicken was cold, and the cat, offended by her expletive, was nowhere around.

"Now Dora, no need for jealous now," said Dr. Apodictou, "Cat is not here now."

"Why did you have to feed it? You knew I wanted to talk to you. Do you feed every animal that walks into this dining room? Do you feed the ducks, the swans? The deer, maybe?"

"Piling up my credits with cat. Investment for future. Thomas Gray is great scholar. I am struggle with possible fake document of nineteenth century. She has great smell for such thing. Maybe she give me trail. Who knows? Talk to me, Dora. I need to clear my mind to zero."

"You know, George, if I'd ordered pie, you'd have gotten it right in the face."

"Well, as it say, no good deed go unpunished."

II

In the Fitzwilliam

Not very far from Pembroke College, the great Fitzwilliam Museum at Cambridge presents its classic but technology-eroded facade to the traffic rumbling down Trumpington Street. The Fitz is one of the great museums of the world with collections in many departments and with several items that are of especial interest to the present story. For example, the keen museum goer will observe the portrait of William Laud, Archbishop of Canterbury (1573–1645), in the gallery at the head of the main staircase. The portrait shows a man of some considerable character, to say the least; but whatever the skill of the artist in delineating this character, the portrait is so little in demand that post cards are not available in the gift shop.

The keen museum goer will probably not be aware of the irony that Laud was the man who arranged for Sir Kenelm Digby's books to be deposited in the Bodleian, that he was the man who hassled the East Anglican Puritans out of England and into New England, and that his career ended by severance—of his head from his neck—for treason. It is not recorded, whether, like the cats of ancient Sabaea, the head of William Laud then spoke up and prophesied.

On a morning with a mackerel sky, rather early, before the tourists had finished their breakfasts of eggs, sausages, broiled tomatoes and cold mushrooms, before the local residents had bicycled to work, Thomas Gray made her way across the street and entered the museum by means of privileged passages available only to those of a certain size.

Without much hesitation, she walked to the section on ancient Egyptian archaeology located in the basement, sat down before the mummy of a XXVIth Dynasty cat, and communed:

Oh, venerable, respected, and perhaps deified Ancestress, servant of the great cat goddess Bastet. Oh, body of a cat soaked in nitre, preserved with honey and spices and pitch, and packaged in linen strips; you remind me of one of those stuffed grape-leaf things that are the speciality of the Mykonos Restaurant on St. Andrew's Street. It is a commonplace that the quick are in better shape than the dead, even though your shell will last for millennia and mine is already touched by a spot of arthritis. So let me celebrate while I am alive and am not yet a residue; for mummy is become merchandise, Mizraim cures wounds, and Pharaoh is sold for balsams.

It is not possible, said the great Einstein, for us to communicate with the past, though it is possible for the past to communicate with us through those evidences of continuity that constitute history. So I commune with you in this way and I hope to learn.

The subject of today's musings is not mortality, but communication. The experimentations of Dr. Redding, a fine young gentleman who may yet learn to transcend his enthusiasms, gave me the shakes. I tell you this frankly. He misinterpreted my reactions, but that is his problem and not mine. What meanings to ascribe to things when Meaning itself is now for sale in the market place?

Each age, Ancestress mine, is a private age and speaks a private language. The kind of thing that was in your head is not in my head, even though we are both cats. For starters, you had no bicycles to contend with. Reciprocally, I, here in Cambridge, or even in Waterfen St. Willow, have no crocodiles to contend with. Try as hard as I can, with the help of historians and archaeologists and anthropologists, I cannot begin to understand what was in the minds of the ancient ritualists. Why, not far from intellectual Alexandria, were cats sacrificed to the god Horus? And why was it that your defunct body was put into aromatic wraps?

Each individual is a private individual and speaks a private language. No one knows for sure what is in the mind of another or how that other mind operates, whether it be that of a cat or that of a human. The assumption of similarities and the possibility of communication evolve simultaneously, and out of this mixture grows public language.

The private language is the crucible in which individuality is brewed. The public language is where that individuality is broadcast. Both are necessary for sanity. Without the public, the private becomes an autism, and though autisms, may contain, for all we know, unique and valuable perceptions of the world, those perceptions are sterile if they cannot be vented. Without the private vision, the public language falls into banality and tedium.

We cats, oh shell of a revered Ancestress, have a reputation for individuality that must be maintained. We communicate publicly, but only up to a point and in limited ways. Our real

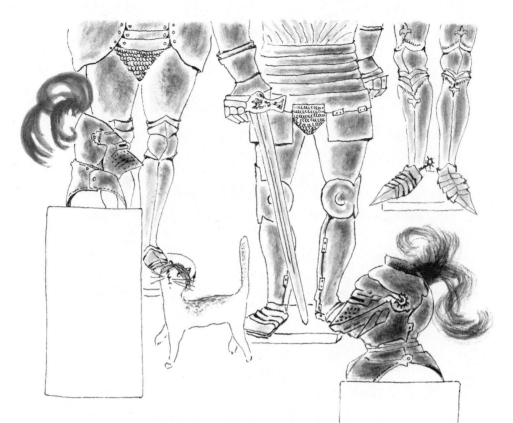

names, as the poet from St. Louis observed, we keep private. To open up our private world to public scrutiny is to destroy our uniqueness and to destroy the possibility of our individual contributions.

And if for cats, then for the Queen; and if for the Queen, then for the Whole Universe which, conceived as a whole, is private and only communicates publicly when it has a mind to.

To know all is to destroy all.

Having unburdened herself of these musings, Thomas Gray waited a moment, as though she expected an answer from her

Egyptian Ancestress. But answer came there none. Her secret exit required that she pass through the gallery where men in armour were exhibited; and as she paused and briefly examined the contents of the cases, she wondered which of today's furnishings either of body or of mind in a few short years would call up buckets of laughter.

12
———

Demitasse

A motley group of Pembroke Fellows was having lunch in the Dining Hall. Lord Eftsoons, Master of Pembroke, and Vice-Chancellor of the University was among them. Scanning the long oak table he made out amongst the group Dr. Lucas Fysst, Professor Adrian Longwood-Beach, looking rather raggle taggle that day, Dr. George Apodictou, and Roderick Haselmere, the Bursar.

The main dish served up was a shepherd's pie; ample, ample quantities of it. The meal was finished off with a blanc mange; ample, ample quantities of it. The large, traditional wheel of Stilton cheese occupied a position of honour at the centre of the table and was pushed back and forth. The Stilton, especially supplied to the College by one and the same cheesemaking family since the year 1771, was at the peak of perfection; id est, it verged on the rotten but was not quite vermicular, and it sent forth an aroma that to a happy few was a Preview of Paradise.

After lunch at table, the company adjourned to the Senior

Common Room for demitasse. Professor Longwood-Beach asked the Common Room at large what had become of Professor Sir Alfred Bowen of Jesus.

"Is he dead, or is he merely revising?"

Roderick Haselmere, the Bursar, replied that he had just read that Bowen had left Jesus and was serving with a European Parliamentary Commission in Brussels.

George Apodictou, in a voice that boomed through the entire Common Room, ventured an interpretation: "It was inevitable, Sir. Those who can, do; those who cannot, move up a metalevel. It is a Law of The Universe. It is for All Time."

Lord Eftsoons approached Lucas Fysst for a private conversation.

"Well, Fysst, I hear it rumoured about that you've had a bit of a triumph."

"Nothing, really, Master."

"Yes of course, Fysst, nothing really. But great honour for Pembroke and all that. Great honour. Call in the London papers, shall we? Make a bit of a splash, shall we?"

"I think not, Master."

At this point in their conversation, Thomas Gray wandered into the room, unnoticed by the two men, and sat down within earshot in a deep leather chair.

"Come, come, Fysst. Modesty's not what's wanted on such a grand occasion. Once in a lifetime, what? We must cultivate our 'nothing reallys'. Beat some drums, wave some flags about, what?"

"Really, Master, I must demur."

"An impediment, perhaps?"

"Thomas Gray, Master, the college cat. She must share the honour with me, sir. She was the sine qua non of the whole enterprise."

"The sine qua non, Fysst? A cat, Fysst? My dear Padre, are you well? A spot too much, perhaps, of the College Curry, if it was curry?"

"You have summed up the problem very well, Master. The assertion of the sine-qua-non-ness, if you will permit the insertion of a philosophical concept, of the cat, would imply, to the commonality of intelligences who read the London papers, that the whole enterprise was the product of an overheated, Bedlamite imagination."

"Yes, I see your point. Cambridge must not allow any suggestion of. . .yes, yes. But, Dr. Fysst, the solution is simple enough; it stares one in the face, does it not? Forget the damn cat. Don't mention him."

"Her, Master. No. I cannot forget the cat. That would be a betrayal. She is the Cat-Without-Whom-Not."

Thomas Gray got out of the chair and made her way quietly out of the room. She gave the impression of having taken notes.

"Well, Fysst, I'm sure you'll work it out. Great honour for Pembroke. Must run now, you know. Meeting of Heads of Colleges. A thought: come to the Master's Lodge any night this week. We shall have a whiskey and work it out. Whiskey is the *omnium solvium*, the universal solvent, if you get my meaning."

13

Le Blanquefort

The *Guide Michelin* does not sprinkle its stars over English restaurants with great liberality; nonetheless, it has scattered some about, and Le Blanquefort, a stone's throw from Buckingham Palace in London, has managed to garner a few. Dr. Lucas Fysst, in the course of his normal work week, is not a very likely person to be found eating lunch in such a place, but on the Thursday following the conversation just recorded, Dr. Fysst was in London, dressed rather spiffily, and at 1:00 P.M. was waiting in Le Blanquefort for the arrival of one Jackson Evans from New York City. He was there in response to a trunk call from London the morning before.

"Professor *Fisst?*"

"Yes? Well, Doctor, actually."

"This is Jackson Evans of Lyman and Lyman, Publishers, in New York. I'm sure you must have heard of Jackson Evans Books, a wholly autonomous subsidiary of Lyman and Lyman? I'm at your service, sir. Lyman and Lyman distributes widely in the U.K. through W. D. Smith and other quality book outlets. I'm pretty sure we must hit Heffer's Bookstore at your place."

"I don't think I've heard of your company. Oh, yes, I remember now. You're the firm that's putting out that new translation of Sextus Empiricus' *Against the Arithmeticians.*"

"I think you've got your wires crossed, Doctor. Maybe you're thinking of *The Secret Numbers of Helena Rubinstein*, based on new documents, and we've just signed Daphne Dhu for a bio-package with CBS. Anyway, to cut through the fat and get directly to the point of the nub, I hear you've got a great human interest story sitting right in your pocket."

"I'm afraid I don't understand."

"I mean your cat. The cat that does research."

"Well. Yes. She. . .I mean. . . .It's all too. . . .Very personal, you know."

"It's a great story, Professor. Could take off like a rocket. We play it for Brains and Tears. A smash combo. Very sensitive treatment. Thelma Thong is all set to write it. Can't keep her away from it. Very sensitive treatment. She's good with Animals. Perceptive. You remember what she did with Keery Kee, the Educated Rooster."

"I could not forget. I never knew."

"Look, Professor. What say we have lunch tomorrow at the Blanquefort. My treat. We can jaw jaw about the way I see this thing moving. When Thelma says she'll take something on, you're talking money in the bank, spelled M – O – N – E – Y."

"Well, thank you very much indeed. I had planned to be at the British Museum tomorrow morning. I'll be glad to accept your invitation."

"One must eat lunch, I suppose," Lucas Fysst thought to himself.

"Great, Professor. See you tomorrow. One P.M. at

the Blanquefort. It's in the yellow pages. Near the Queen."

At 1:10, a cheerful, pumpkin- faced man of medium height pushed through the rotating door of Le Blanquefort, and looked around for someone who was looking around for him. In this way, Evans found Fysst and, initially confused by Fysst's collar, recouped, slapped him on the back cordially, linked arms and said, "Well, I see you're a Member of the Alms Services. That's a joke, son."

"Yes. I'm in orders. However, I do no pastoral work. I'm a historian of science."

"What an angle! What an angle for TV. Dark shirt, white collar, Harris tweed coat. Great relief from the fat tie Salvation Slingers; stateside, that is. Real Quality here."

The manager of the restaurant approached and Jackson Evans gave him a similar treatment.

"Henri," he said, slapping him on the back, "long time no see. You look great. Making lots of *pyenyenza*, I hope? How about a nice table for the Professor here and me?"

"Ah, Meestair Evans! Where have you been all zees long time? We have meesed you. I have always say to mon boss 'Meestair Evans whan he comes in he makes again ze springtime in ze heart'."

Henri snapped his fingers. The Captain approached, recognized Jackson Evans and received his orders from Henri.

"Antoine! I wouldn't know you. You've moved up in the world."

"Oui, Monsieur Evans. No longer to be a waiter. I have made ze advancement to Capitaine."

The two men were seated and two huge menus were thrust in front of their noses.

The Sommelier approached.

Jackson Evans thrust his menu aside and said to the waiter

confidentially, "The usual, Philippe. And another for the Professor."

"Yes sir, Mr. Evans. Two usuals."

"Well, let's get to the heart of the nub, shall we? Take a look at this contract I had worked up in New York."

Jackson Evans hauled out two copies of a document and gave one copy to his guest.

" 'AN AGREEMENT between Lyman and Lyman, of New York, New York, hereinafter known as "The Publisher", and Professor Lucas Fysst of Pembroke College, Cambridge, hereinafter known as "The Author". . . .' Blah blah. Of course, you're not the author. Thelma is the author. I mean the writer. Legal nicety. Let's skip all that. . . .'For a work tentatively called *The Cat that Beat Einstein*, hereinafter known as "The Work". . . .' Standard stuff. Royalty 10% for sales up to 5,000 copies, 12.5% up to 50,000, 15% thereafter. Blah blah dah. Standard stuff. . . .Let's get to the interesting part."

"If you don't mind, I should like to call The Work, if the work eventuates, and I have reservations, *The Sine-Qua Cat*."

"Yes. Yes. Terrific title. I'll take it to Thelma. Her titles are always on the button. She's a million dollar baby in a five

and ten cent store. Woollie's over here. Now let's see. Here's
some more blah blah. Standard stuff. Let's get down to where
the action is: 'Section Six. Subsidiary Rights and Peripherals'."

The Hors d'Oeuvre Waiter rolled his laden wagon up to the
table and asked, "Messieurs would like to try of ze saumon fumé?
Cured in especial way for Le Blanquefort. En Écosse, vous savez."

"What was it cured of?" asked Jackson Evans.

"Very good. Monsieur Evans makes ze good joke."

"Cured of Original Sin, I should think," Lucas Fysst ventured, "which is possible for Scotch salmon but not for humans."

"Ha ha. Monsieur le curé also makes ze good joke."

"Foreign rights. Blah blah dah standard stuff. Now what
we are proposing here is this: A five-way package deal between
you, me, that is, Lyman and Lyman, Argus Cable, and Data-
Animation in LA. You're talking no fewer than five personal
appearances in the States plus two taped one hundred fifty second
splits, plus—now get this—plus five book promos in New York,
Philadelphia, Denver, Miami Beach and Scottsdale, Arizona;
plus—get this—plus a hookin with the Daphne Dhu promo.
Remind me to query if she's sensitive to cats, else we hire a
stand-in.

"And if it flies, a Call-in Show later on where the cat gives
personal and intimate advice. This whole package—got it?—we
hand over lock, stock, and barrel to Cal-Ouse Productions, while
controlling the artistic say-so and integrity, keeping the costs
down and royalties and subsidiaries up. Right?"

"Let me understand, Mr. Evans. I'm getting the impression
that you are not here as the representative of Lyman and Lyman.
You are, how shall I put it, an agent?"

"I am Jackson Evans of Jackson Evans Books. Wholly autonomous subsidiary. We work directly under the umbrella of—
friendly cooperation with—Lyman and Lyman and Argus Cable.
We navigate artistic projects through the complicated financial

and contractual waters that are inevitable in today's high tech world. Right?"

The food waiter approached.

"Louis! You are now a waiter? No longer hewing and hauling?"

"No. Mr. Evans, I have made ze advancement."

"That's great. Just great. Advancement is what makes the world go round. Well, I'll have the usual."

"Yes Mr. Evans. One usual. I find out what is zis usual. And Monsieur?"

"And I think I'll have something comfortable. Something familiar. A nice quiet curry ought to do it. Yes, I should like a nice comfortable curry," said Lucas.

"A curry, Monsieur? Here in Le Blanquefort? It is not possible a curry. Monsieur should like, please, to make examine la carte?"

"Oh, no curry? In that case, why don't you just bring me another usual."

"Oui. Two usuals."

The production of the usuals involved three assistants who mixed liqueurs, set them on fire with razzle dazzle flourishes of napkins and silver salvers, and then did things with thin slices of meat. All through the entrée, Jackson Evans carried out a monologue, dwelling entirely on Section Six.

As they were finishing up, the captain came over and asked whether all was in order.

"A-one, Antoine. A-one."

The Captain then addressed Lucas Fysst. "And how did Monsieur find everyzing?"

"It was superb. The fish was superb."

"Ze fish, Monsieur? Fish? But Monsieur had ze veal!"

"Veal? Oh yes. Veal. So it was. I meant. . . .What I meant to say was that, of course, in this restaurant, everything is so superb that it all tastes the same. No. What I meant to say was. . ."

A fury of monstrous proportions rose in the Captain.

"Bon Dieu! Quel crétin! Quel barbare!" he burst out, directing his anger towards a nearby aspic, and shaking the trolley so vehemently that the noble jelly trembled and began to resolve itself into its constituent fluids.

"Monsieur," he added politely when he had calmed down, "we are listed in ze *Guide Michelin*!"

Jackson Evans continued with his monologue. Towards 2:40 P.M. Lucas Fysst got restless. High Life in Kensington produced symptoms of distress unrelievable by calcium carbonate or magnesium hydroxide.

"I think that what you propose is unlikely. Thomas Gray is a very private individual. I was under a misapprehension. I thought it just possible that under your aegis the Eudemus story might be brought to a slightly wider audience than would be the case with professional publications."

"What distresses me," Fysst continued, "is that you don't seem to realize my work must have some inner consistency, some coherence. It's not produced on demand, either with or without your Thelma. It must be part of an oeuvre. History must judge it as an oeuvre."

"Sleep on it, Professor. Thelma Thong is number ten on the sensitivity scale."

14

Th'applause of List'ning Senates to Command

June tenth, the day of the presentation of the honorary degrees at Cambridge. A very light rain was falling. Umbrellas were opened and closed, opened and closed. There was great buzz in the ancient streets. The college flags flew and a helicopter in the skies above beat its wings. Ladies and gentlemen in quite formal attire, ushers in top hats and swallowtail coats, college porters in derby hats, dons in polychromatic regalia thronged the area in front of the Senate House. On the streets outside the iron fence there were tourists, bicyclists, shopkeepers, and greengrocers from the nearby open market. Cameras flashed and TV trucks pulled up to record the events.

Bobbies and security men galore patrolled the area, for the honorary degrees would be presented by the Chancellor of the University, and the Chancellor was Prince Philip, the Duke of Edinburgh. He would be accompanied by the current Vice-Chancellor, Lord Eftsoons, the Master of Pembroke, but Lord Eftsoons, as we shall soon see, would not have to say a single, solitary word in the ritual that followed.

An academic procession formed outside the Senate House and paraded around the quardrangle before entering the building. His Royal Highness, the Chancellor, was preceded by the Esquire Bedells, each carrying a silver-knobbed mace. The Prince was clad in a gorgeous cap and gown of black and gold and was followed by a page who carried the train of his gown. Then came the University Marshall in a blue uniform decorated with brass and medals.

Next in line were the recipients of the honorary degrees, referred to as the graduands. The graduands were followed by the Registary, the Vice-Chancellor, the Proctors, the High Steward, his deputy, the Commissary, the Heads of Colleges and the Regius Professors. Then came Lucius Fysst, gowned in a robe of red, and following him, all the lesser fry in the University pond.

As the procession marched around the quadrangle, a peal of 720 changes rang out from the bell tower of the adjacent Church of St. Mary the Great. Five musicians entered the Senate House first, and then the choir boys of King's College Chapel, dressed in red suits and white collars underneath black robes. They made their way through the center aisle and to the gallery. The Chancellor took his place on a magnificent red velvet chair placed on the dais. He sat down, and then the whole congregation sat down.

The Senior Proctor announced that the honorary degrees would be presented. The University Orator arose and stood to the right of the Chancellor. Each graduand was approached by a proctor and escorted to a place before the Chancellor. The graduand stood there while the Orator read out the citation, in Latin and with dramatic intonations.

The Chancellor then rose, and with his lines written out for him in red, pronounced (and occasionally mispronounced) a for-

mula in Latin. He shook hands with the graduand. The audience
applauded, and the newly-created honorary doctor took a seat on
the dais behind the Chancellor and the Vice-Chancellor.

In this way, Sir John Arthur Makefield-Prentice, Lord George
Frederick William Campbell Stuart, Dame Felicia Angelsea
Cornwall, and the Reverend Stanley Otis Stanley, were presented
and doctorified.

Three more graduands were yet to be presented. The Vice-
Chancellor observed that the Chancellor was tapping his foot, for
the Songs of Praise sung out by the Orator were, to put it delicately, slightly, ever so slightly, tedious. The Vice-Chancellor
tried to catch the eye of the orator and to indicate to him to
speed it up, for Heaven's sake.

There was a slight pause while the Orator shuffled some
papers. Then, there was a stir in the audience. All eyes were
turned to the steps leading up to the dais. What was going on?
A small gray and white object was mounting those steps. Who
or what was it? It was Thomas Gray, the Pembroke Cat. And
she proceeded to stage center where she faced the Chancellor and
then sat down.

The audience tittered. The dignitaries frowned. How did a
cat get in? All eyes now turned to the Chancellor. A broad smile
broke over his face. After all, if a cat may look at a king, a
Chancellor may certainly look at a cat.

"Fortunate are they who can perceive the causes of things"
is a quotation from Vergil that has been carved into the walls of
Churchill College; but more fortunate still are they who can bloody
well perceive what to do about them.

Such a man was Ian Dunbar, Lord Eftsoons, Master of Pembroke and Vice-Chancellor of the University. The Vice-Chancellor rose, approached the Orator, and had a word with him. He

went back to his seat. The Orator approached an Esquire Bedell and had a word with him. The beadle approached the cat, apparently to have a word with her, but at this point Thomas Gray stepped forward slightly and paused momentarily. Then she ran off to the left and disappeared.

The audience reacted with smiles, with laughter, cheers, applause, whistles, and stamping of feet.

The remainder of the ceremony went forward without problems or interruption, with calm and dignity, and at the recessional, the peal of bells from St. Mary the Great was said by old timers to have been unusually long and vigorous.

Angst

15

The Disappearance

The Presentation of the Honorary Degrees had come and gone. The Footlight Revue, that yearly satirical production, written and acted by undergraduates, some of whom, in past years, have gone on to great successes in movies and television, had come and gone. The May Balls—young men dressed in white ties and tails, young ladies dressed in light taffetas—had come and gone. The Bumps—those strange races upon the River Cam—had come and gone. The graduations at the individual colleges had come and gone. Parents had pulled up their cars on side streets and loaded them with books and clothes and hi-fi equipment, and now these had come and gone.

The college quadrangles, deserted by students and by dons, were taken over by groups of tourists, swarming like bees, who were lectured to by their group leaders in half a hundred languages.

"Here," the guide would say, "is the room where the great Isaac Newton lived. Here is the entry where the spies lived. Bolted to Moscow, you know. This is the portrait of Professor J. J.

Thomson, who discovered the electron. Mind the step as we go out. Now the very walls of that college over there harboured a nunnery in the twelfth century.

"In this college John Harvard once lived. Harvard College in New England was named after him, you know. Also Oliver Cromwell lived here. Hotbed of Puritanism, you know. This chapel is the only one in the University with a cruciform floor plan. Here is the entry where E. M. Forster lived. The writer-chap who did all those movies. Honorary Fellow."

"Here is the spot where more than two centuries ago there was a large basin, and Roger Long, the Master of Pembroke, paddled around it in a water velocipede."

The Bursar of Pembroke and his staff, catching up now on the odd jobs that had been deferred to the slow season, laboured on. One of the secretaries noticed out of the corner of her eyes that Thomas Gray, the Pembroke cat, seemed a bit out of sorts. She was heard to miaow every now and then, plaintively, and there was no apparent reason for it. She seemed restless, and she couldn't get herself organized. Lucas Fysst reported that she no longer came to his rooms at teatime. She no longer was seen walking up Trumpington Street toward Market Hill.

The cat took a turn for the worse. She refused her food. Tidbits were brought from the food stalls—for what cat's averse to fish?—and she turned them down. The Bursar remarked that this state of affairs could not go on and said that the next day he would take her to the animal hospital. But on the morning of the next day, Thomas Gray was not to be found.

A search party was sent out to explore all her known haunts and it came back after an unsuccessful expedition. The Porter called the Cambridge Police and the Police answered that they were not equipped to handle enquiries about missing cats. Most of them, the Police added with cruel laughter, were run over by cars.

The Bursar was devastated. The little dishes outside his office remained full but bereft of meaning; his morning ritual of supervising her chow was reduced to dust and ashes. Arthur Darby, the Head Cook, about to set out on holiday, asked the Bursar whether he should bring back a new cat; a kitten perhaps. "You know, to make it cheerful like," he added but the Bursar couldn't answer.

There were only a few Fellows around; those who were heard the news. "Bad business," Dr. J. M. D. Redding remarked to Dr. George Apodictou, Reader in Byzantine History. "Sad business," he responded in a loud voice, "and I had an appointment to consult with her."

Dr. Lucas Fysst heard the news and camouflaged his grief with a scholarly diagnosis couched in classical language. *"Consuetudo peregrinandi,"* he said, "the habit of wandering is endemic in cats."

Lord Eftsoons, having returned from Cefalù where he and Lady Eftsoons were recuperating from their graduation duties, heard the news. He rang up the Bursar immediately. "Sad. Very sad," he said, blowing his nose into his handkerchief with a mighty and authoritative blast.

An hour later, the Master encountered Adrian Longwood-Beach in the quadrangle, and when Longwood-Beach thoughtlessly said "Pussy cat, pussy cat where have you been, eh Ian?", the Master gave Longwood-Beach such a look of total disapproval that the latter sank into the ground, so to speak, and, like Job, cursed the day wherein he was born, so to speak.

Then rumours started to come in. It was stated that Thomas Gray had been observed in the early morning in the chapel of Jesus College, looking up at the memorial to another Thomas, that of Thomas Cranmer, first Protestant Archbishop of Canterbury, molder of the Anglican Church and burned for heresy. She was said to be filling the apse with odd sounds.

It was stated with equal authority that she had been observed near Churchill College, sitting near the house in which Wittgenstein lived and looking up at the window of the room in which he died. These rumours proved hard to disprove.

And then the rumours became an exercise of wit. It was asserted that Thomas Gray was in Westminister acting as adviser to a select committee of Parliament; and it was asserted equally that she was in Washington as an éminence grise for economic policy.

At this stage, of course, she became a national and an international figure. Her picture was run in the papers and on television; for after all, here was a cat of considerable reputation at the University of Cambridge. Some readers, thinking foolishly that there must be a large reward posted for the return of this famous personage, came forward with all manner of gray and white cats, of which there are quite a few in England, and tried to palm them off as Thomas Gray.

In the U.S.S.R., the official newspaper Pravda suggested that Thomas Gray had been kidnapped by the C.I.A., as she had intuitive knowledge about new mathematical methods in cryptography. MI5 and MI6 got involved, and at Question Time, the Prime Minister stated in Parliament that a long tradition extending back several years forbade her from commenting publicly on security matters.

In Deal, a man set forth on a raft christened "Thomas Gray", and proposed to cross over to Norway. In Piccadilly, Thomas Gray T-shirts were being hawked. Blackwell's book store in Oxford reported at 535% increase in the sales of the *Collected Poems of Thomas Gray*; in the United States, Lyman and Lyman, publishers, were said to be rushing into print with a no-holds-barred biography, but no one was certain whether the cat or the poet was meant.

Back in Pembroke College, everyone was sad. Sad, but hopeful. Work slowed down. Repairs that were scheduled to be done over the summer were just not getting under way. There was an undeclared mourning and it was disruptive. Even auxiliary services were affected. The installations of new telephones by British Telecom were strangely delayed.

At long last, when it seemed that all avenues had been explored and all reports sifted and evaluated, Lord Eftsoons, the Master of Pembroke, gave word that the flag of Pembroke bearing its coat of arms be lowered to half mast for the period of one hour.

"Let us all get on with it," he said poignantly, and his remark was widely quoted and approved.

16

Philosophers at
Waterfen St. Willow

he River Cam, rising near the intersection of the
A1 and the A505, flows through the City of Cambridge, past the Isle of Ely and its magnificent ca-
thedral, and northward till it meets or becomes the
River Great Ouse. On its distinguished, but hardly
broad, surface, one may find racing sculls, rowboats, canoes, punts,
motor boats, pleasure boats, houseboats, and occasionally a barge.
In years gone by, there was a considerable barge traffic up the
river from King's Lynn, but this is no longer the case.

In the V formed by the Cam and the Great Ouse, between
the villages of Welney and Southery, is situated the small village
of Waterfen St. Willow. Far from the madding crowd, the inhabitants of Waterfen tend fields of wheat, potatoes, market veg-
etables, and berries. There is a church of no great architectural
merit or historical significance. It bears the name, in modified
form, of St. Willaloe, who flourished in the area in the eighth

century. Inside the church, there is a marble tablet displaying the names of the clergymen who held the living (strangely, in the gift of All Soul's College, Oxford) from 1784 to 1921. There is also an elaborate coffin with effigies in painted plaster of the Earl of Fennismere and his wife (He: 1591 – 1663. She: 1603 – 1648).

The village has a pub, the Hare and Sluice, whose lunches are of such high quality that they attract diners from as far away as Peterborough and King's Lynn. The local residents swear at the pub for having created a traffic problem where such a problem never existed, and by any stretch of logic, should never be permitted to exist.

The village has a gift shop kept by a woman who makes and sells corn dollies. These are little figures of women, about six inches high, made of blades of wheat. The figures have their origin in pagan magic, the theory being that a spirit of fertility dwells in a wheat field, and when the wheat is harvested, the spirit will die unless it is preserved in little images made from the last sheaves cut.

The village has neither a public telephone nor a public convenience.

About a year after the events in the Senate House recorded here, in the break between terms, Dr. J. M. D. Redding, of quasi-fragment fame, borrowed a motor boat owned by his neighbour G. Peebles, intending to have a bit of a holiday on the waterways of East Anglia. Redding had no children, and his wife, Margot, was in New Zealand visiting her sister.

Redding got to the area of Waterfen St. Willow and proposed to have lunch at the Hare and Sluice, whose reputation was even then spreading to Cambridge. The tower of St. Willow's was visible from the river, so he tied his boat to the trunk of a tree and headed for the village several miles off along a dirt road. On this occasion, he ordered fish and chips augmented by two half pints of bitter. For a sweet he ordered a dish of gooseberry fool. This lunch was rather more than he generally had, but then, he felt expansive on the occasion of his twofold freedom.

Upon leaving the pub, Dr. Redding saw, or thought he saw, a small gray and white animal, possibly a cat, run out from between two houses on the main street and into the churchyard. It disappeared in the uncut grass between the graves.

"My goodness," Dr. Redding thought to himself, "that cat, if it is a cat, resembles Thomas Gray quite closely. I wonder whether it is Thomas Gray." And he resolved that when he returned to Cambridge from his holiday, he would take the matter up with Lucas Fysst.

Back from holiday, he broached the subject to Fysst, who questioned him closely.

"What colour was it, John?"

"It was gray and white, mostly white. I mean to say that the side I saw was gray and white. I saw only one side, you see. One must be quite careful in reporting what one sees."

"Yes, I see. And the side you saw, what side would that have been?"

"It would have been the side on the right, assuming you face the head of the animal directly on."

"On its right or on my right?"

"On your right."

"And did that right side, beginning at the top, exhibit a slight tendency towards a gray wash, ever slighter as one proceeds toward the underbelly?

"It did."

"And did the animal have gray or white socks on, so to speak. I mean on its right side, of course."

"White socks."

"It must be Thomas! It must be she! I shall go as soon as I can break away. One more thing, and this is of some consequence. At what time in the afternoon, approximately, did the animal rush toward to churchyard?"

"Between 1:30 and 1:45."

"It must indeed be she."

"Assuming it was a cat."

"What other animal might it have been?"

"I make no hypotheses as to that."

The two men took leave. But something else occurred to Lucas Fysst as he was on the staircase.

"John. One more thing. It really is important. When you were in the pub, were you served by a waitress?"

"Yes."

"Could you identify her?"

"Well, she was wearing a black uniform and a white apron."

"Would that serve to identify her uniquely?"

"Probably not. I suppose all the girls wore black dresses with white aprons. But she wrote her name on the back of the bill."

"American fashion."

"Precisely. St. Willow is not a backwater, you know. They haven't yet come to the transatlantic terminology of waitpersons, but she did write down her name. Billy or Brenda or Bobbie. It began with a *B*. 'Billie is serving you.' That sort of thing."

Borrowing, or rather, sub-borrowing the boat of G. Peebles, Lucas Fysst set out the next morning for Waterfen St. Willow. Knowing that Thomas Gray tended to be a creature of habit with a rather rigid schedule, and being quite alert to the methodology of experimentation, he thought that his chances of duplicating J. M. D. Redding's results would be increased

greatly if he duplicated closely J. M. D
Redding's procedure.

He sailed or putt-putted down the Cam
towards Waterfen St. Willow. When he
spied the church tower, he attached the
boat to a convenient tree. This took
him rather a bit more time than he
had allowed, for he had never before hitched a boat to the trunk of
a tree. He then walked to the Hare
and Sluice.

"Would there be a waitress here
whose name is Billie or Bobby or
Brenda?"

The young lady he addressed shook
her head.

"Would there be a waitress here
whose name begins with a *B*?"

"Would Barbara do?"

"Yes, Barbara. Very logical
name. Ha ha. Academic witticism.
Aristotelian, actually."

"You one of those dotty fellows
from the University?"

Lucas Fysst blushed. Outspoken little
thing, he thought to himself.

"Are you Barbara? I should like to be
served by a lady whose name begins with a *B*."

"Sit here, luv. The items we have today
are all on that blackboard. And blackboard begins with *B*. Just
like in a classroom. And classroom begins with a *C*."

He ordered the fish and chips, though he would have preferred the curry, and two half pints of bitter; and for a sweet, he ordered a gooseberry fool.

"Thank you, sir, but we don't have gooseberry fool today. Would a nice peach fool do?"

"Damn. Sorry. No, it won't. Yes, of course it will. Peach fool, then."

"Thank you, sir, and peach begins with a *P*."

"Thank you, Barbara. I've come to find a gray and white cat. I hope my routine will elicit the cat."

"I'm sure it will, sir. Fools always do, sir."

At 1:30, precisely, Lucas Fysst exited from the Hare and Sluice, stood in front of the pub and waited. One forty-five passed and no cat, or other animal, ran out from between two houses and into the churchyard. The church clock struck two and still no animal.

He walked around the little village and saw nothing. Cats, rabbits, birds, yes; Thomas Gray, no. He resolved on one more strategy. He went to the middle of the churchyard and selected a large, horizontal weather- and lichen-stained slab. He sat down, and with the area thus staked out, very much like Sherlock Holmes and Watson on one of their rural cases, he waited.

The sky darkened, and Lucas Fysst's stomach rumbled a bit. Teatime came. Then, about ten feet away, there was a slight rustling in the grass. The tall blades parted, and tentatively, Thomas Gray poked her head out and looked around. She walked over to Lucas Fysst and rubbed up against his leg. He called her his Pangur Bán and took a cube of Turkish delight out of his pocket and offered it to her.

17

At Evensong

Lucas Fysst and Thomas Gray sat together at dusk in the country churchyard; in the silent intuition that binds those who have loved one another, Thomas conveyed her thoughts:

"When I was young and green, I was full of the pride of my own brilliance, and full of the ambition to display and augment my brilliance. I did not want my flower to blush unseen. I therefore went to Cambridge at the suggestion of the Elders and with the approval of the Community.

"In Cambridge, I found many who were wiser than I. Initially, this was a shock, for coming from a small village that embodied a limited view and limited experience, it was very easy to believe myself Top Cat in the world. Nonetheless, I persevered at Cambridge, worked hard, raised a family en passant, and swallowing my pride, I listened and learned from whatever source I could. I made great progress. I advanced rapidly. I began to see the larger world and to understand my position in it a little better.

"Then came success—great success—at a relatively early age, really. And when you walked to the Senate House, garbed magnificently, I followed you there—largely out of curiosity. And when I realized what was going on inside, my breast swelled and my head grew large. And I imagined that I too might be honoured on that platform and before that audience. I imagined that I stood there, robed in the glorious academic colours, like a tropical bird, and the University Orator called out in a loud voice:

'PRESENTO VOBIS FELEM PLEBEAM SED AMANTEM AMAN-DAMQUE ERUDITISSIMAM ET MAGNANIMAM AD GRADUM ASCEN-DENDUM MAGISTRAE SCIENTIARUM HONORIS CAUSA THOMAM GRAY COLLEGII PEMBROCHIANI SOCIAM TRANSITORIAM.'

"And since the printed program could not have carried these unexpected words, the Orator rendered them into English:

'I present to you, for the degree of Master of Science, honoris causa, a cat, of average descent, as cats descend, who is most friendly, most beloved, most learned, and of a most elevated spirit: Thomas Gray, Visiting Fellow of Pembroke College.'

"Yes, indeed, I thought. Praise me; I can stand it.

"And then, in my imagination, even as these words of praise were being recited, even as I was standing in front of the Chancellor receiving my honour, I felt pangs of doubt. I asked myself what was in the hearts of my fellow graduands. Had they achieved what they really wanted or hoped to achieve, or were they being honoured for what they themselves regarded as almost accidental and almost paltry.

"And for each person who stood erect on the dais, there were ten others, a hundred others, who equally well might have been honoured for achievements no less significant than the ones celebrated. What was in their hearts?

"Success brought me to depression. In the first place, there were no more worlds for me to conquer, for having achieved the highest honours I could imagine, to duplicate them once, twice, or more would have added no luster to my reputation. Secondly, I began to feel that my intellectual success was in no wise due to any conscious effort on my part; that it was due to the working out of a vast, impersonal, world machinery that might, with equal ease, have cast me exclusively in the role of mouser in a remote village cottage or in the dessicated attics of Pembroke.

"Here was a second blow to my pride: that for all my brilliance, I could not with any consistency achieve what I wanted to achieve and that my brilliance could not with any consistency be instrumental in changing the world in ways in which I perceived it ought to be changed. The paths of glory had led but to ambiguity.

"I do not deny the existence of extraordinary genius. I acknowledge it and I revel in it. But one must also not deny the fact that isolated genius is an impossibility; that great Newton of Trinity College stood on the shoulders of giants and the giants drew the meaning of their achievements from the commonality of language and experience that constitutes civilization. But what can a civilization do, the whole of it, to honor and to celebrate its own existence?

"Then, there was something else bothering me. Rather different. Some day I'll tell you about it. . . .

"At any rate, I resolved to go back where I came from to spend a season or two thinking through my Cambridge experience. In many ways, life is much simpler in Waterfen St. Willow and provides an opportunity to simplify and to analyze. I was taken in by a cheerful, elderly couple who raise fruit and ship it to the jam factories. They are not exasperated when I have one of my moody episodes and my back goes up.

"Mevrouw has passed on and I have taken over some of her consulting duties. I am delighted that you have looked for me and found me and obviously believe that we could work together again. I don't know whether I want to return to Cambridge. Let's just say that it's an option I'd like to keep open."

In the western sky the downward sun sent forth its last effulgence. It was now twilight. Man and animal separated. Each went his own way, Thomas Gray toward the village houses and Lucas Fysst toward the church. The church was open, but no one was in it. He found some matches and lit two pew candles, one on each side of the aisle, and set their glasses back in place. The church filled with pale light that created dark and deep shadows.

"Oh Pangur Bán," he cried, "Pangur Bán,

> Practice every day has made
> Pangur perfect in her trade
> I get wisdom day and night
> Turning darkness into light."

And then, to round out an evensong of his own strange devising, Lucas Fysst intoned the Psalm of David:

"Dominus illuminatio mea et salvatio"

in plainsong, moving backwards slowly towards the door as he sang, and he stepped onto the porch and into the dark village leaving the interior of the church illuminated, but empty.

18

Mésalliance?

*I*f the cat would not come to Cambridge, then Cambridge would come to the cat. It was inevitable. However, what is inevitable often comes about indirectly.

A few day after Lucas and Thomas Gray were reunited, Lucas received a small package in his Pembroke mail with an enclosed note.

Dear Dr. Fysst:

I got your name and address from the enclosed day book which I think you left at the Hare and Sluice.

Is your name pronounced like fist or like Christ?

We have another batch of gooseberries and we shall have fool all week. I make it.

Sincerely yours, B.

This letter received an immediate answer.

Dear B:

Which I very much hope stands for Barbara.

I was enormously relieved to get my diary back. I am quite lost without it, you know. Rather like glasses. I wouldn't know when to show up or where. Most embarrassing. I can't thank you enough.

Your indirect suggestion that I order gooseberry fool is a good one as it might reduce the time required to materialize Thomas Gray, the cat.

My name rhymes with 'diced'. Your rhyme, though correct, might be construed as unnecessarily irreverent.

There are two separate theories as to where my name comes from. Some hold it is a shortened and variant spelling of 'fissting', an Old English word that means a small mongrel dog. I assume that one of my remote ancestors must have been small and quarrelsome. I am neither.

Others hold that it is derived from 'feist', an old German word meaning fat or plump. I prefer the second as the first has some disagreeable subderivations.

Sorry for being tedious, but as Disraeli said, I have a tendency always to reduce steam engines to tea kettles.

Yours faithfully,

L. Fysst

In its turn, this letter received an immediate reply:

Dear Lucas Fysst:

I should have told you that your cat lives with Pa, Ma, and me. Pa owns a fruit farm very near to the Hare and Sluice. I suppose you'd like the cat back. I can't guarantee delivery because it's not always around. It is very independent.

Sincerely yours,
Barbara

And the last of this series was:

Dear Barbara: No. I do not want Thomas back. She must live her own life. However, I shall visit her, and hope I may visit you as well.

Yours faithfully,
Lucas Fysst

Lucas Fysst made many trips to Waterfen St. Willow to visit his friend whom the world called Thomas Gray and whom he called his Pangur Bán. Each time he went, he followed the same routine: lunch at the Hare and Sluice at Barbara's table, followed, after an appropriate lapse of time, by a reunion with Thomas. The gooseberry fool reappeared in good supply. It was ordered and eaten, and the cat reappeared at 1:30, proving that the Whole Universe follows the laws of physics once those laws are sufficiently fine tuned.

As the number of visits increased, Lucas thought of Barbara less as a syllogism and more as a woman. Barbara, for her part, thought of Lucas less as a fool and more as one of God's innocents who would be strengthened if he touched earth occasionally.

The inevitable happened: Lucas found that he was spending less and less time with Thomas Gray. And if he spent less and less time with Thomas, he spent more and more time with Barbara. They explored the fen villages (in her car) which, for all the time he had spent in nearby Cambridge, he hardly knew:

Wisbech, Holbeach, Downham Market, King's Lynn. They borrowed a boat and went along the rivers and canals. Barbara taught Lucas to drive, and he practised his driving over the empty spaces of the beautiful rolling County of Norfolk.

As they drove, often in exhilarating silence, Barbara took stock, for she knew she was coming to a time of decision. Luke is a man, she thought, who eats with gusto but rarely notices what he eats or what he wears. He told me that one morning he put on two shirts without being aware of it. He cannot look at a signpost on the road without going back into ancient history. He detests politics (which I rather enjoy), and thinks that the present must be allowed to ripen for five hundred years before it can be savoured.

He shares his honours with a cat — is he really dotty? — and seems to have been able to talk his colleagues into similar marks of respect.

At the same time, he is kind, loving, forthright, devout (in his way) and steady; he dazzles me with stories that describe worlds I never knew existed. He tells me about gods and devils, numbers and squares, scholars and geniuses and eccentrics, and when he does, he glows, he glistens with excitement and happiness, and I think: here is the phosphorescence of learning, here is all the magic of *The Thousand and One Nights* in my right hand.

Bring Luke down from the clouds? Can't be done; and even if it were possible, what a waste! The fellows from Lynn come to the pub in groups of twos and threes with snappy talk about yachts in Malta and with an eye on the main chance. The whole world comes to The Hare. I've dealt with them all. The earth is full of men who merely creep along its crust, and to add one more to their number is not what is wanted.

A don's wife? It's not what I dreamed of when I read *The*

Secret Garden, but why not? The little soirées at Cambridge, the concerts and all the clever talk? Could I fit in with it ? Yes, why not?

He said to me once in a quite offhand way, quoting Scripture, which he doesn't often do, that therefore shall a man leave his father and mother and cleave to his wife, and they shall be one flesh. But not one mind, he added, he should not like that.

And will he cleave to me, or is he hopelessly wed to his manuscripts and his fantasies? Wed, yes; hopelessly, no.

Will it work out? Why shouldn't I work it out? It's not going to be served up on a silver platter, is it now?

Thus Barbara. And Thomas? During this season of courtship, Thomas seemed to have been demoted to the role of just another barnyard animal who took her meals with the ducks and the chickens. For her part, she was withdrawn and remote; she was pensive and she looked worried.

Lucas thought of having banns posted, and independently, Barbara did also. But neither told the other, and each wondered whether the common part of their individual worlds could ever consist of more than the shared love of a cat and of the magical universe the cat evoked.

Resolution

19

At the Arkesdens

The home of William and Caroline Arkesden, fruit farmers in Waterfen St. Willow, was being readied for an occasion of some importance. Dr. Lucas Fysst, Fellow of Pembroke College, was invited for lunch, and the thought was—it was an unspoken thought, of course—that this was the day on which the question would be popped.

The meal was set for Wednesday at 1:00 P.M. On the preceding days, there was much shopping, much polishing, much straightening out, much cooking. William Arkesden, a handsome man with a military bearing, knowledgeable and successful, carried himself particularly tall as he surveyed his planted acres and thought that he might shortly be losing the apple of his eye.

Caroline Arkesden, setting in the roast, said what a pity it was that Young William could not be there to meet the nice Dr. Fysst.

"Well, that's the Merchant Navy, isn't it. He's Somewhere

in the World," responded William Arkesden by way of consolation.

"We should at least have invited Auntie Lorrie. Dr. Fysst would like her. She always runs the jumble sale at St. Phillips."

"Errumph."

At 12:30, Dr. Fysst, wearing tweeds and a collar, arrived bearing a bottle of double malt for Mr. Arkesden and a large box of chocolates for the ladies. William Arkesden, dressed smartly in a blue blazer, accepted the gifts for the household, saying that the women were poking around in the kitchen somewhere, don't you know, and proposed a bit of a drink of health's sake.

"A splendid idea," said Lucas, rubbing his hands together, and they raised their glasses in a toast to the future.

"Incidentally," said William Arkesden, who was an outspoken man, "How shall I call you? Dr. Fysst? Reverend? Professor?"

"Goodness. I am not a professor. Not yet, at least. I should think that Luke would do."

Mr. Arkesden reminisced about his schooldays at the Abbey School at Ely and mentioned a half dozen names, none of which Lucas recognized. They started on a second drink and then were called to the table.

The handsome rosewood dining table, as Mr. Arkesden pointed out, had been built by Mr. Arkesden's great grandfather as a masterpiece upon completion of his apprenticeship as a cabinet maker. It was set with the family china, silver, crystal, and napery.

The meal itself, done up by Mrs. Arkesden and her daughter, was splendid: roast beef, Yorkshire pudding, potatoes, green beans, and at the end, a dish of gooseberries.

"Do have some double cream with the berries, Bishop," said Caroline, "It makes them so good."

"Call the Reverend 'Luke', Mother. He's not old enough for a bishop."

Thomas Gray walked into the dining room and sat down on the rug.

After the berries were finished, cheese and biscuits were pushed around the table, while the four diners politely and desperately tried to break new ground for conversation.

"You know," said Mrs. Arkesden finally, "When the Queen is at Sandringham over a weekend, she often goes to church in Sandringham Village."

"Very nice lady, I've heard," said Dr. Fysst.

"Very nice. And the Queen Mother is very nice."

"Yes. Very nice."

Mr. and Mrs. Arkesden made their excuses. Lucas and Barbara took their coffee outdoors and sat down by the vegetable garden. In the distance, they could see pleasure boats moving along the river that flowed in an elevated channel above the level of the fields. Thomas Gray came out to join them.

"Ah Pangur Bán! What a grand meal we have had. And have you had your share?"

"Why do you call her Pangur Bán, Luke? Who was Pangur Bán?"

"Pangur Bán was a cat who lived in the ninth century. He was the pet of an Irish scholar or monk in a monastery in Southern Germany. The cat is mentioned in a very beautiful Old Irish poem that describes their life together. It contrasts the life of a scholar with that of his cat. Their life together was not unlike my own life with Thomas Gray has been."

"Has been?"

"Has been. But I hope it won't be for much longer. Oh Barbara. Will you marry me? What do you say?"

"I say yes, silly."

"Shall I ask the permission of your father in proper Victorian fashion?"

"You may, but he's already spread the news in The Hare and Sluice."

"Have I been so transparent?"

"Like water. But before we go inside, tell me who wrote the poem."

"No one knows. It's a mystery."

20

Passion Examined

Some days after the grand meal at the Arkesdens', Lucas and Barbara returned to her house after a drive through the fens. Suddenly she said to him, "Luke, tell me about Pangur Bán."

"Do you mean about Thomas Gray, the cat?"

"No. I mean about the Irish poem."

"Do you really want to hear all I've put together? I'm not an Irish scholar, you know, but I've collected a few facts that interested me."

"Yes. Tell me."

Lucas took this as an invitation to present a bit of a lecture. Now he was in his element, and he lectured with zest.

"Sometime before the middle of the 1800s, a German historian and literary scholar by the name of Franz Joseph Mone, the Director of the Grand Ducal Archives of Baden, (or, as he would have said himself, Direktor des grossherzoglichen Badischen General-Landesarchives), discovered a manuscript in the library of the Monastery of St. Paul near Wolfsberg in southern Austria (actually, it's in northern Yugoslavia now) which set the community of Celtic scholars abuzz for some years. The manuscript, now referred to as *Codex Sancti Pauli LXXXIV*, contained what was then the earliest known example of secular Irish writing.

"Mone reported his findings to a number of Celtic scholars including one Whitley Stokes. In a letter to Stokes written in January 1859, Mone stated that the manuscript came originally from yet another monastery, that of Augia Dives (or Reichenau), which sits on a small island in the western arm of the Lake of Constance. It's well known that in the eight and ninth centuries, the Monastery of Reichenau was popular with Irish monks. Over the years, the contents of the manuscript were published in the *Zeitschrift für Celtische Philologie* and other such learned journals.

"What was in the manuscript? A variety of odds and ends, and this led to the conjecture that it was the writer's scrap book. Bits of Greek grammar; a few thoughts about Cicero; many well-known Latin Hymns for the canonical hours: vespers, evensong; a few lines of Vergil's *Aeneid*; a few fragments of astronomy mentioning Eratosthenes and Archimedes; a bit of formal logic mentioning the system of Boethius. Last, but far from least, there was a collection of five Irish poems or fragments.

"I got on to the manuscript because of its astronomical fragments. Western astronomical material is rare in this period. It turned out to be nothing at all. The poems were far more interesting.

"One of the poems was a drinking song eulogizing Aedh, the son of Diarmait, the son of Muiredach, a chief in the north of the ancient kingdom of Leinster in Ireland. This fits in with the dating of the manuscript.

"Another poem, complete in itself, absolutely unknown, was the lovely one about Pangur Bán, the cat who was the pet of a monk. That poem raised the scholars' eyebrows a half inch or so, and has induced many contemporary poets to make translations. It elevated the Monastery of St. Paul to great heights in the collective mind of the community of students of Old Irish, which, a century and a half ago, I would guess amounted to a half-dozen people.

"The conjecture is that the author of Pangur Bán was a monk from the Kingdom of Leinster in Ireland who wandered to the Monastery of Reichenau on an island in the Lake of Constance

and spent some time there. It's well known that monks often had pets. Some scholars have conjectured that the cat was an Irish cat taken along on his journey by the monk. That sounds unlikely. Cats wander, yes. *Consuetudo peregrinandi.* But most cats hate to be boxed up and carted.

"What does Pangur Bán mean? No one really knows. 'Bán' means 'white'; so the white Pangur. Some have conjectured that 'Pangur' means 'furry'. So 'furry white'. All this on the assumption that the monk called his cat by a Celtic name. But the manuscript seems to have been written in Reichenau, a long way from Ireland. What was to prevent him from adopting a local cat and calling him by a local name?

"The manuscript, of course, had to be deciphered, transcribed and translated. After all, ninth century Irish handwriting is not like today's handwriting. There were some problems of paleography. And in those days, separation of the letters into words was not done or was done erratically.

"One of the authorities who worked on the poem was a fellow by the name of Heinrich Zimmer. Zimmer published a version of the Irish text in the *Glossae Hibernicae* in which the words 'Pangur Bán' are rendered as 'Pan Gurban'—the letters grouped differently, you see—and then proceeded to interpret the poem in an entirely different way.

"Zimmer suggested that the words 'Pan Gurban' are not Irish. They are Slavic and mean 'Mr. Hunchback'. According to Zimmer's theory, Pangur Bán was not a cat at all, but a man!

"One then supposes that Zimmer interpreted the references to mouse hunting and all that in a metaphorical way—the wit of the Middle Ages, perhaps—whilst the monk was engaged in important intellectual matters, Mr. Hunchback, a clod, was wasting his time with trivialities.

"This unpleasant theory was destroyed in October, 1881 by

a refreshing blast of cool, sensible thought from the pen of Whitley Stokes writing from the Indian resort town of Simla. Whitley Stokes was a great Celtic scholar, but made his living from the law. At one point he was President of the Indian Law Commission.

"Ah, for the days when scholars were men of independent means; when the pursuit of scholarship was separated from the necessity of earning one's bread and butter. No insect in the Ministry of Education asking you for the social justification of what you're doing. A concept of devotion to learning for the spirit of man and to the glory of God. No guilt. No guilt. I hear that in America nothing happens without competing for a grant. No grant, you can't flush the loo. But this is grousing. Extraneous to the story.

"Stokes wrote to the *Révue celtique* and said that Zimmer is totally mistaken. He is ignorant of the simplest facts of Irish metre. He does not realize that the metre of the poem is what is called *deibide*. This means 'split in two' and it calls for a monosyllable at the end of the first half of each line and a dissyllable or a trisyllable at the end of the second half. (In our English renditions, each line of the original has been split in two.) If he had remembered this, he would never have made such a stupid mistake.

"Whitley Stokes didn't let it go at that. Apparently old Zimmer was a rather nasty fellow who had just roasted an older scholar, E. Windisch, unnecessarily. Whitley Stokes was an equally nasty fellow, roasting everybody, and suggested that Zimmer had revived the days when rival scholars and theologians called each other dirty names in Latin—pigs and worse things. And he wound up his letter by saying that if Zimmer would just please learn a little more Irish he'd be in better shape.

"Over a long career, a typically Victorian career with a tremendous output, Whitley Stokes himself made many mistakes of the sort he castigated Zimmer for. He patched them up quietly. He knew when he was wrong.

"To sum it all up. Who was the monk? Was the monk identical to the poet? What does 'Pangur' mean? Where is the manuscript? Sitting in a glass case for visitors to St. Paul's to admire between the hours of 10:30 and 3:00? I don't know, and I should like to."

"You mean," said Barbara when the lecture was over, "that a cat, a mouse, and a monk, hundreds of years ago, have led you to all this?"

"You forget scholars. Cats are not the only ones who are curious."

"Are these things important to know?" Barbara asked.

"Important? Not in the sense that Whitehall is going to base a policy on the knowledge or that the knowledge will lead British Leyland to a splendid new product. But it matters to me.

"It's a mystery, and I want to know the answer. The desire to know can become a passion. I don't even know that it is possible to know, and that intensifies the mystery. Perhaps the knowledge is irrevocably lost. On the other hand, it might just be the case that there is a person, somewhere in the world, who can simply reach into his bookshelf and pull down a document in which the answers are all spelled out neatly and completely.

"I've had numerous passions, and this may become another. I've fed of the dainties that are bred in a book, have eaten paper, as it were, have drunk ink. Books and manuscripts are my passion, and the mysteries contained in them. Passions inflame, but a life lived without passion, without desire, is a life that's not worth living."

Barbara listened to Luke and said quietly, "I should think that too much knowledge might spoil a poem."

Thomas Gray listened to this conversation and thought to herself:

"He has got his quote wrong. It's the *unexamined* life that's not worth living. Socrates taught us that. Examined passion? Now there's a paradox. Passion that's examined is lost. It vanishes like the mist over the morning fens.

"Unexamined passion may lead to disaster; I've heard many instances of it. Each evening before I tuck in, I pray that the world may be saved from its zealots, its saints, and other manifestations of excessive passion.

"Talk, talk, talk. All that history-besotted lad does is talk, talk, talk. When will he get on with it and take the lass in his arms? He is shy. Ashamed before me, I daresay. I shall discover a mythical mouse and chase after it. That should accelerate matters."

Thomas Gray ran into the fields. When she returned, she found the couple in a deep embrace.

"Hah," she thought. "In the case of the present display of zeal, I shall make an exception to my general rule."

Over the next several weeks, Thomas Gray sensed that Lucas and Barbara were joining their individual worlds. She felt that she had been replaced in their affections by each other and by a paper cat, centuries old. She was therefore doubly redundant, and once again she disappeared.

21

The Unchewed Cud of Learning

*L*ater that evening, back in his rooms at Pembroke College, Lucas Fysst pulled on his pipe and thought about his life and his work.

What does my constant poking and grubbing among books and manuscripts amount to? Of what relevance to today's life is my store of information about the past, its ideas, its personalities, its events? Why should I call up dead spirits from the vasty deep and bid them testify?

I know that many, even among my colleagues, think me antiquarian, conservative, stagnant. I am perceived walking the streets wearing a wig and a cocked hat. My opinions vis-à-vis the latest national sensation are held to be obscurantist, provincial, puritanical. My concerns with the minutiae of the past, concerns that give me so much pleasure and that illuminate the condition of man in a way that makes it endurable for me are held to be nit-picking or evidence of a crabbed mind turned upon itself. My concern with language and with the truths that lie buried within language are held of no account.

Sweep the closets clean, I hear them saying. Sweep out Fysst. Let's clear the bridge for action. Fysst and his crowd are not civilization as they sometimes claim, they are roadblocks to civilization; panhandling, sponging, carping, supernumerary, self-isolated, monastical roadblocks to progress.

Why should I not quit my chambers immediately, reset my calendar and my watch to this year, this day, this minute, and go out into the world beyond the ivy and the lamp. I could comfort those who are hurt and bring the message of God's Kingdom to the downcast.

Yes. It's a possibility. It does not contravene the laws of physics. But it is not what I want to do; it is not what I'm good at doing.

And anyway, in the long run, what does my work really matter? In the long run, as John Maynard Keynes of Kings pointed out in a gloss on the basic notions of the Theory of Probability, in the long run we are all dead.

O Blessed Lord,
thou hast given me horses, books, Cambridge, and
peace:
foolish the man, having these, who seeks increase.

But wait.

Over the centuries, many men have sat within the noncon-formist gates of Cambridge, while their consciences have wrestled with their experience and their experience has wrestled with their heritage. Wasn't Cambridge the cradle of the Protestant Reformation in England? Wasn't it the seedbed of an alternate vision?

Yes, many men. Start with Cranmer and Ridley and Latimer: Cambridge men. Burned at the stake for heresy in the tragic times of Bloody Mary. And Nicholas Ridley was the Master of Pembroke.

A hundred years ago, troubled inquiry overtook William Kingdom Clifford, Trinity, the great mathematician, and Leslie Stephen, the critic, and led them to agnosticism. Yes, of course, of course: include Charles Darwin, who lived in digs on Fitzwilliam Street just yards from here. All of these men were made ill by their struggle and suffered greatly.

Then there was Henry Sidgwick, Trinity, the philosopher of ethics. He found he couldn't subscribe to the Articles of Faith and left until the religious test was removed. Maynard Keynes said that Sidgwick never did anything but wonder whether Christianity was true and prove it wasn't and hope it was. This doubt flowed directly to those philosophers of mathematics who spent their time wondering whether mathematics was true and proving it wasn't and hoping it was.

Within memory, E. M. Forster sat in his rooms in Kings and pondered which was the least odious: to betray his friend or betray his country. Now there's the history of science in a nutshell: betrayal of an ancient faith by allegiance to a new vision.

I do not have the problems of these men. My problem of conscience is different: how can I take flight from the world and justify my life as a scholar in an age that clamours for the destruction of the University. Of what value are my studies of the fourth century (and sometimes the ninth) in an age that regards action as primary, an age that opts for quick returns, for the now, for the life of sensation?

What is the proper function of a University? A question that has confronted us from Socrates to Augustine, and from Augustine to John Henry Newman, and from Newman to Alfred

North Whitehead and to the latest white paper issued in London
by the Ministry of Education.

Of course the University must be, in part, of this world. I
make no objection to its laboratories, its courses on business
strategy. Lord knows that the University has contributed its share
to this world. Atomic energy, that simultaneous blessing and
curse, was a University product pure and simple, born in a University garage out of University conceptualizations.

And now, well into the atomic age, the increasing mathe-
matizations that have come about through the computer, bring-
ing with them a mixed blessing of another variety, have crystallized
out of the spirit of logical inquiry. Here is another University product, and its spirit can be traced in a path from the Egyptian
scribes of four thousand years ago, through Pythagoras and Euclid,
through Archimedes and Ptolemy. There is a straight line that
passes from the cells of the mediaeval grammarians and logicians
to the sweatshops of software and the ateliers of Silicon Valley.

It's clear to me that the University must serve many pur-
poses; a vocational purpose and a social purpose and a community
purpose. It must, of course, advance learning. It must provide a
common language of intellectual discourse. But there is one purpose that is threatened, and that is the purpose that justifies my
existence within this community of practical people.

The metronome of change is set at presto prestissimo. It
sweeps us into frenzied movement. So much is already known
and so much new is discovered each day that it is beyond the
ability of any one person to accommodate it all. We become
unbalanced. We reel and are swept away. The glut of information that calls itself knowledge sates us and creates nausea; the
glut of knowledge that masquerades as wisdom creates despair.
We are teased by the possibilities of automated thought. Like

Faust, we are seduced by the promise of Mephistopheles that if
only we abdicate thought, we shall gain all thought; we shall be
saved and find ourselves, like innocents, back in the Garden.
Mindless in Paradise.

But the University is the place, par excellence, where people
have thought and must think. If given proper nourishment, the
thoughts of youth can be long, long thoughts. It is fitting and
proper that their thoughts be hard and solid and deep.

We are confronted everywhere by the unchewed cud of
learning. We teach procedures and not meaning. Our philosophers, who represent the conscience of thought itself, like hos-
tages commanded to dig their own graves prior to execution, are
asked to prepare evaluations of their own cost effectiveness. Our
priests, who might ease the heart's sadness by enabling the spirit
to transcend the finite, are demeaned by politics and jumble sales.

The University is the place where the cud of learning must
be chewed. Slowly. Lento lentissimo; and the men and women
who supervise these ruminations and who judge them must show
the way by dedicating their lives to them. Not learning for its
own sake; not knowledge for its own sake, but to invest facts
with all their possibilities. Not in isolation from the world, but
so that these studies and introspections may convert the products
of the human mind into instruments of civilization.

Four centuries ago, Queen Elizabeth I came to Cambridge
and apostrophized my college:

"O domus antiqua et religiosa!"

I like to think that in a secular age, passion for thought and
devotion to thought, modulated by that paradoxical fellowship
of faith and skepticism, must be the continuation of the Queen's
perception.

22

Simulations

King's Lynn, a pleasant town of some thirty thousand people, growing rapidly now that the M11 has brought it much closer to London, sits near the mouth of the River Great Ouse, thirty miles from Waterfen St. Willow. King's Lynn is an old town, known to the Saxons and the Danes. Its church of St. Margaret dates from the twelfth century and has magnificent brasses that tourists love to come and rub.

In mediaeval times, the town was known as Lenne Episcopi. When Henry the Eighth had finished with the bishops, its name was changed to Lenne Regis. Most people call it just plain Lynn. There is a market square, cleared of cars on Tuesdays, the market day. The Coffee Shop of the Dukes Head Hotel on the square provides excellent fish and chips and a ploughman's lunch, while its dining room can supply the most fastidious with sumptuous fare served in a elegant setting. The dock area is charming and numerous buildings from the seventeenth and eighteenth centuries have been preserved. The visitor will find reminders that George Vancouver, the famous explorer of the Pacific Ocean was a native of King's Lynn and that the novelist Fanny Burney was born across the street from St. Margaret's where her father was organist.

To King's Lynn, then, on a bright Saturday morning, Barbara and Lucas came looking for Thomas Gray. They had no particular plan; they would spend the morning in Lynn and look, just as they had looked in other places.

They parked near St. Margaret's and walked up High Street, reserved for pedestrians, past H. Samuel, Jeweler, past Marks and Spencer, past the newly-opened Macdonald's where Supermacs were now available. They walked into Market Place, sat down at a sidewalk cafe and had coffee and scones. They thought next to walk down to the quais just opposite, when they saw a number of young men in the hairdos of primitive American Indians. Feathers and all.

"This punk styling, or whatever it's called," said Lucas, "is rather much, you know. How civilization seems to retrogress. And the earrings that men are wearing now. The other day I crossed at the lights near Parker's Piece. An enormous lorry pulled up and the brute of a driver was wearing an earring. It must have a meaning, but the meaning escapes me. In seventh century Assyria—B.C. that is—men wore golden earrings. The fashion was limited to kings and their court."

Barbara said that when punks wandered into the Hare and Sluice, they generally spoke very softly.

They walked down King Street and more Indians appeared. A man on horseback in the uniform of an eighteenth century British officer crossed their path.

"There must be an outdoor do of some kind," Barbara said.

"Let's find it."

They found it at the Square near the old Custom House. The whole square had been taken over by a TV company shooting a picture. The square was swarming with actors, extras, makeup people, directors, grips, script women, wardrobe people, camera crews, and huge vans containing electrical generators. Outdoor lights, wind machines, and smoke machines were set in place.

A moment's thought and Lucas realized what was going on: the dock area of Revolutionary Boston, Massachusetts had been recreated in the dock area of King's Lynn, as it was probably as close a replica of historical Boston as still existed. To the historical buildings of King's Lynn carpenters had added detached parts of ships' masts and hulls, facades of thatched roof houses, a stock, and a gallows. They had salted and peppered the area with signs that read "Thomas Cabot, Horse Shoeing", "Richard Dunster, Silversmith", "To Concord, 9 Miles".

To this huge outdoor set, the general populace of King's Lynn was admitted freely, and shoppers lined up in multitudes behind containing ropes.

"What's going on here?" Barbara asked her neighbour.

"Why, they're making 'Her Loyal Heart' with Daphne Dhu and Cary Carradine. And Daphne Dhu's sitting right out there on the next street!"

"Carrie Carradine? Who's she?" Lucas Fysst asked.

"He, silly. He won an Academy Award last year for 'Bolts and Nails'."

"Must have been riveting. Absolutely."

They walked along the periphery of the ropes, when lo, even as predicted, Daphne Dhu, in eighteenth century hoopskirts and décolleté that·displayed an abundance of her well-publicized parameters, was sitting in the back seat of her open white Rolls

Royce, smoking a cigarette and playing patience on a little port-
able table set up in the street. She was quite approachable and
autographed whatever people shoved in front of her: a shopping
bag or the back of a letter.

Lucas Fysst came close and raised his voice towards her. "By
any chance, Miss, have you seen a gray and white cat?"

Daphne looked up and saw that her questioner wore tweeds
and a collar. "Dearie. In my day, I've seen hundreds of gray and
white cats. And some purple ones as well."

"Yes, of course you have. Very logical of you. What I mean
is. . .oh, dash it."

"Not very accommodating, was she?" said Lucas later.

"Should she have been?"

The crowd now moved en masse to where the cameras were
located. In a moment, shooting would begin.

An assistant swept the horse pats away. The streets were
hosed down. The lights were lit. Large reflectors were adjusted.
The wind machine was started. The smoke machine was started
(to simulate a shop that was being burned down, no doubt). The
sound apparatus was in place. Young extras poked their heads
and hands into the stocks. Actor-beggars displayed limbs painted
with simulated blood. Defiant householders poked their heads
out of the windows of two-dimensional cottages in simulated rage.

A special effects man lit a pile of straw wet down to burn
longer. An actress-whore sashayed down the reconstructed Colo-
nial street proudly displaying the letter *A* sewed onto the breast
of her dress.

A sudden query from the script coordinator: "The letter *A*
bit. Anachronism, possibly?" Pause. Then a voice from somewhere on a bullhorn: "It's O.K., Basil. No problem. Roll now."

A red-coated officer in a powdered wig and a three-cornered
hat walked onto a platform and read the Riot Act. Three officers

on horseback rode down the street rapidly. The simulated rabble moved back toward the houses in simulated fear. A single file of Indians in war regalia followed the riders, whooping and making threatening gestures.

"Cut. Retake."

A red-coated officer in a powdered wig and a three-cornered hat walked onto a platform and read the Riot Act. Three officers on horseback rode down the street rapidly. The simulated rabble moved back in simulated fear. A single file of Indians in war regalia followed the riders, whooping and making threatening gestures.

"Cut. Reloading camera."

Then, once again, a red-coated officer in a powdered wig and a three-cornered hat walked onto a platform and read the Riot Act. Three officers on horseback rode down the street rapidly. The simulated rabble moved back in simulated fear. A single file of Indians in war regalia followed the riders, whooping and making threatening gestures.

In all of this, Daphne Dhu had no part. She sat patiently, as she had learned to do and had done for thousands of hours, playing patience and smoking. She waited for her five minutes under the lights.

Barbara and Lucas watched a simulated world repeat itself. Twice. Three times. Four times. Five times. The film would be run down to London, processed, run back, and the director would make his selection from a dozen takes.

On the last retake, a gray and white cat ran across the street in front of the horses. It lost itself in the general chaos.

"Thomas Gray!" Barbara shouted.

"Could it have been? It happened so suddenly. I couldn't really see."

Whoever it was, whatever it was, it was now preserved on

film. For posterity. *In saecula saeculorum.* Maybe. If it didn't end up on the cutting floor.

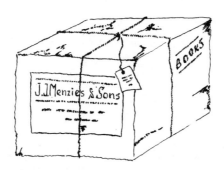

23

George's Help

ne morning, some months later, not too early, around 11:42 A.M., in fact, Dr. George Apodictou rang up Lucas Fysst.

"Lucas, you get to my house right away. I have a thing to show you. Right away. Yes. 15A Maryanne Close."

Now hearing was obeying when Dr. Apodictou was concerned, so Lucas pedalled over to 15A Maryanne Close and presented himself at the door.

"Good. You are here. You know the beautiful Daphne Dhu? No? Yes? You shall know. But she is a small aspect. I spin you a latest cassette 'Her Loyal Heart' to a certain place and you must watch. Now you sit here. So."

"I've met Daphne Dhu," said Lucas.

"Is so? I also. What you think?"

The action began. A red-coated officer in a powdered wig

and a three-cornered hat walked onto a platform and read the Riot Act. Three officers on horseback rode down the street rapidly. The simulated rabble moved back toward the houses in simulated fear. A single file of Indians in war regalia followed the riders, whooping and making threatening gestures.

"I do not understand logic of Indian sequence but watch now closely."

A gray and white cat ran across the street in front of the horses.

"Look at what we see. Look at cat. It is definitively Thomas Gray. It must be. I stop picture and reshow frame by frame."

"Yes, it's she. It has to be. Notice the white socks and the gray cap. I shall go immediately and get her. But it's been months. It's been months."

Then George Apodictou said,

"But that film was made in Boston, America, New England! You will go to America? I think Thomas Gray is become famous cat actress. Our Pembroke famous cat is now great Hollywood actress. What a career! Quelle artiste!"

"No, George. She must be here in King's Lynn. Don't ask me how I know, but I know. Great coincidence. In our business great coincidences are everyday affairs. You should know that. I'm going immediately. I should have followed it up months ago."

24

Final Dialogue

Lucas Fysst bicycled to the Cambridge railroad station and took the next train to King's Lynn. He arrived about three o'clock and went immediately to the churchyard of St. Margaret's. He waited.

The afternoon wore on. The glimmering landscape faded. Fewer and fewer people trod the streets. The air became distinctly chilly. The smell of the sea was in it. A bell struck the half hour. Thomas Gray emerged from the shadows pushing back the tufts of grass near one of the gravestones and walked directly to Lucas.

"Ah, Pangur Bán. You bad cat. You ungrateful cat. You cat who won't be confined. You cat without whom I'd have nothing: no reputation, no wife, no sense of the deep mysteries that envelop the world. Where have you been?"

"I have been to sea," she informed Lucas in their private language, "and I go there again tonight, for I have experienced the terror of the infinite. I have desired it and have not yet had my fill. And of this, I shall now inform you.

"A long time ago, when Mevrouw interviewed me, she asked me about very large numbers. I gave her a slippery answer. I am sure that if I had answered her in a straightforward manner, her next request would have been: now tell me something about infinity. That was lucky for me, because at that time I had no thoughts on the matter. I was pretty green. And then, after I went to Cambridge, I remembered a story that my grandmother Katrina (on my mother's side) told me.

"When Katrina was young she took a job as ship's cat on a scow operating out of King's Lynn. Not one of your noble boats but experience plays no favourites. One day she was sitting on the bridge looking out at the water. The scow was somewhere out on The Wash far from land. There was a stiff breeze and the surface was choppy. She could see hundreds of little wavelets. First the wavelets formed and then they collapsed. Above in the sky, seabirds flapped their wings, and far off, very far off on the horizon, another vessel was just barely visible.

"Suddenly Katrina's eye caught a single wavelet that had just then reflected the sunlight. The wavelet was visible for an instant; then it collapsed and disappeared. And she realized that she had experienced a *specific* wavelet out of myriads of wavelets that have formed and unformed on the surface of the ocean since the oceans themselves were born. And she realized that although she could assert the existence of that *specific* wavelet her eye had picked out, and although someone standing beside her might also have experienced it and might bear witness to it, there was now no way in which she could make its specificity palpable. The specific had collapsed and had dissolved itself into the general.

"Katrina told me that when she thought about this transformation she was terrified, and she said her terror was far greater than that of Pascal contemplating the eternal silence of infinite space. The dissolution of the specific, she said, was the death of art.

"I thought about her story over and over again in my own way and what I concluded was this: that infinity must be located in the gap between the specific and the general. And I thought moreover that if mathematics is the science of infinity, as some claim it is, its regenerative powers must be located in that gap. And that when mathematics puts forth its definitions and tries to capture infinity in its net, at just that point infinity slips away and is replaced by the finite.

"The word 'definition', after all, comes from *definio*, meaning: I enclose within limits, I fix, I finitize. Once something has been defined, it is like cats' meat: we may prepare it and feed on it, and we require it to nourish us; but it is dead matter.

"I needed time to think about all this. It troubled me. I went to Lynn and signed on as ship's cat on a scow, hoping to duplicate my Gran's career. I wanted to see whether I could experience her feelings. I sat on the bridge and watched the waves break and disappear; and their individual character was eternally lost. And her terror came over me and I knew that I had experienced something without knowing what it was.

"My soul thirsts for that which is and yet cannot be known in its entirety. I have tasted it and have not yet had my fill. When I do, if I do, I shall forget the bitter waves. I shall forget the booming breakers and the harsh, fish-reeking brine. I shall come back to Waterfen St. Willow and be with you. But you mustn't think to confine me and you mustn't grieve when I walk away."

"Ah, Pangur Bán. Who can define a cat?"

And so back in Waterfen St. Willow, the banns were posted

for Barbara and Lucas. Back in the Senior Common Room at Pembroke College, eyebrows were raised when it got noised about that "such unlikely material for marriage", as Professor Sir George Martin put it delicately, had exhibited the primal tendency of life.

Roderick Haselmere, the Bursar, said that wives tended to come out of the fens. *The Chronicles of Pembroke* revealed that a hundred years ago, at the time the celibacy requirement for dons was lifted, ready-made wives and children had come out of the fens.

"Yes indeed. Baldrick, Ranscombe. Then Pilchard, the philosopher. Rather complex fellow, Pilchard. Two separate families came forward. Don't think he ever got his book written."

Thomas Gray spends occasional mornings clearing the strawberry fields of rabbits and afternoons pawing over interpolated palimpsests. From time to time, in the evenings, she thinks about infinity. And from time to time, she is away on extended business of her own devising.

Laus Deo, who, in an age of existentialist interpretation, has allowed a conclusion that is upbeat.

THE END

Acknowledgements

During a recent stay with my wife in Pembroke College, which was delightful in every way, Mr. C. Gilbraith, the Bursar of the College, introduced us to Thomas Gray, the college cat. He told us that one of the Fellows had dedicated a book to her. This introduction and subsequent acquaintance with Thomas was the genesis of the present fantasy.

I should like to thank C. Gilbraith and M. J. D. Powell of Pembroke College for arranging our stay there; and Pembroke College, quite generally, for its splendid hospitality.

Thanks also to Ernest Davis, Joseph Davis, David Joyner, John V. Kelleher, Clara and David Park, David Pingree, Jerome Weiner, and John Wesley for much that was sine qua non.

I am indebted to Edmund Hlawka of the Technische Universität, Vienna, for acquainting me with the Problem of Theodorus of Cyrene by giving me his paper "Gleichverteilung und Quadratwurzelschnecke", *Monatshefte für Mathematik*, 89, 1980, pp. 19–44.

Readers who may be interested in a recent summary of opinions about the Problem of Theodorus are referred to *The Evolution of the Euclidean Elements* by W. R. Knorr, D. Reidel Publishing Co., Dordrecht/Boston, 1975, Chap. III. See also "Theodorus' Irrationality Proof" by R. L. McCabe in the *Mathematics Magazine*, vol. 49, 1976, pp. 201–203. *The Dictionary of Scientific Biography*, Charles Scribners, Vol. XIII, has a nice article on Theodorus by Ivor Bulmer-Thomas.

On the existence of a world that is unobserved, see, e.g., N. D. Mermin, "Is the moon there when nobody looks? Reality and the quantum theory," *Physics Today*, April, 1985, p. 40.

The poem about Pangur has been translated many times and into many languages. For the original Irish version together with a literal translation, see Gerard Murphy, *Early Irish Lyrics, Eighth to Twelfth Century*, Clarendon Press: Oxford, 1956. For other renditions, see Frank O'Connor, *Kings, Lords & Commons*, Alfred Knopf, New York, 1959, and Robin Flower, *The Irish Tradition*, The Clarendon Press: Oxford, 1947. One of Flower's stanzas has been used, with permission, in Chapter XVII. O'Connor's version reproduces something of the original Irish rhyme pattern which is alternately on accented and unaccented syllables.

The words of Mehitabel the cat are taken, with permission, from *Archy and Mehitabel*, Don Marquis, Doubleday and Co., 1927.

The poetic lines in Chapter XXI are taken, with permission, from the play *Thomas Cranmer of Canterbury* by Charles Williams, *Collected Plays*, Oxford University Press, London, 1963.

A good place to read the life of Digby is in *Sir Kenelm Digby*, R. T. Petersson, Harvard University Press, Cambridge, Massachusetts, 1956.

For the poet Thomas Gray, I recommend *Thomas Gray*, R. W. Ketton-Cremer, Cambridge University Press, Cambridge, 1955. For Pembroke College, see *Pembroke College, Cambridge: A Short History*, A. Attwater, Cambridge University Press, Cambridge, 1936.

For Columbus's log book offered for sale, see S. E. Morison, *Admiral of the Ocean Sea*, Little, Brown and Co., Boston, 1942, p. 328.

* * *

I should like to thank the staff of Harcourt Brace Jovanovich for their many courtesies extended to me over the years. This book owes much to the imaginative editorship of Klaus and Alice Peters. They have demonstrated the possibilities of an extraordinary relationship between author and publisher.